CAT TALES:
Fantastic Feline Fiction

MORE FANTASTIC FICTION
FROM WILDSIDE PRESS

Nobody Noticed the Cat
Anne McCaffrey

If Wishes Were Horses
Anne McCaffrey

Fantasy: The Best of the Year
edited by Rich Horton

CAT TALES:
Fantastic Feline Fiction

Edited by George H. Scithers

WILDSIDE PRESS

CAT TALES: FANTASTIC FELINE FICTION

ISBN 978-0-8095-7321-9

Compilation © 2008 by Wildside Press

Introduction © 2008 by George H. Scithers

All stories are original to this collection and are
copyrighted © 2008 to their respective authors
except "The Cats of Ulthar" by H.P. Lovecraft, first
published in 1920; "The Cat" by Charles Baudelaire,
first published in 1857; and "Kreativity for Kats"
© 1961 by Fritz Leiber, reprinted with permission.
Original illustrations pp. 64, 89, 122
© 2008 by George Barr.

Wildside Press
www.wildsidepress.com

For more information, contact
cattales@wildsidepress.com.

CONTENTS

INTRODUCTION

by George H. Scithers

Here are thirteen stories, three haiku, and a conventional poem, all involving cats. A few, like "The Cats of Ulthar" and "Kreativity for Kats," are well-known classics; others, like "Creeper Shadows," are freshly written and came meowing to us in search of a home at *Cat Tales,* 9710 Traville Gateway Dr, #234, Rockville MD 20850 or by e-mail to g-scithers@sff.net. (Do be sure that e-mailed stories include *both* your snail-mail *and* your e-mail addresses.)

Cat Tales: Fantastic Feline Fiction offers a home for many sorts of stories involving cats: fantasy stories, mystery stories, and science-fiction stories — and every so often a story that doesn't quite fit into any of these genres, just to present our readers with the unexpected. We also seek poetry involving cats.

Cat Tales is intended to be a continuing series, rather like a magazine in paperback-book format. Our first volume is devoted mostly to fantasy stories — a deal with the Devil, a re-incarnation, and a long tale of Medieval magic, even a dragon — along with a couple of murders and a science-fiction story. For our next volume, well, let's see who we find purring inside our mailbag.

It's hardly surprising, considering all our fiction involves cats and the people who are owned by them, that so many of our contributors are from the United Kingdom, Canada, Australia, and New Zealand.

While we welcome reprints as well as new stories, we prefer ones that have not been published recently in North America. Do beware of stories whose "cats" are better described as elves, gnomes, or little men who are dressed up in furry costumes and are just pretending to be cats. We and our readers strongly prefer believable cats behaving in believable, cat-like ways, coping with whatever strange things — fantastic, mysterious, or science-fictional — that befall them and their human companions.

Our upper limit is supposed to be around 15,000 words, but can be flexible about that. We want to avoid talking cats (yes, yes, we know: one of the cats in this issue does say six words, but that's a special case — you'll see what we mean) and and to avoid cats coming to a bad end on stage. Think of *Cat Tales* as a place for stories told (or read) by the fireplace with a contented cat purring in your lap.   ❖

NOT ANOTHER BLACK CAT STORY

by Geoffrey Maloney

THE INSTRUCTIONS were quite clear on the website: the cat must be black and it must be dead. The dead black cat must be taken by the tail and dragged gently across the top of a freshly dug grave, care being taken not to awaken the inhabitant within who was sleeping the restless sleep of the newly dead.

The website was one of those ones you come across from time to time . . . the sort you find in a moment of desperate searching late at night, the sort that if you don't capture the information when you see it, then you may never have the opportunity to do so again. Such sites come and go, first giving you access, then denying it, or simply vanishing as if they never existed. Perhaps later, they emerge under a brand new URL to supply their esoteric wisdom to others, giving them the one-time opportunity you, yourself, have missed.

This time, however, I did not miss it. No, in my desperation, I took a pen and clean piece of paper as quickly as I could, and began to write down the precise details of the ritual which needed to be performed. If you are familiar with these types of websites, you will know there is no point in hitting your browser's PRINT icon. Nothing will happen. Your printer may activate as per normal; and a sheet of paper may well scroll through it; but when you take the paper in your hand, you will find that there is nothing printed there, not even a faint outline or an indentation of the words which conveyed the information you sought.

So there was nothing for it, but to archaically transcribe the details by hand. And this, as it turned out, needed to be done swiftly. As soon as I started writing, I found the page on the screen beginning to blur. It faded to grey then, in a green flash, I was confronted by a young woman showing me her breasts. Had I merely been duped into accessing a pornography site? But she *was* wearing a funny red hat that had two cute little devil horns curling out of it. So I believed I'd found what I was looking for. Finding the authentic Devil website had been one thing, but now it seemed I had a bigger problem on my hands. To wit: where does one find a dead black cat in Brisbane?

Despite my shortcomings, and — believe me — I have many, the slaughtering of innocent pets for personal gain is not one of them. No, the truth is I am pacifist who abhors violence of any kind. Honestly, I would not hurt a fly; and, notwithstanding a rational fear of spiders — I was convinced those living in Brisbane were all poisonous — I always managed to usher up enough courage to carefully extradite them from my house and into a habitat more conducive to their ongoing survival. Others, as you know, think nothing of squashing every spider they see between shoe and floor, ignominiously sweeping up the remains and disposing of them down the toilet afterwards.

So you will appreciate my dilemma then. I could not simply go to the pound, the pet shop, or look up the newspaper classifieds, purchase a black cat, bring it home, and strangle or perhaps smother it in some way. No, if I was to purchase a living, breathing cat in this way, I would be more inclined to give it a saucer of milk, stroke it behind the ears, and immediately give

NOT ANOTHER BLACK CAT STORY

it some endearing name. At least in this way, I would have some other creature to share my immediate and present danger with. The alternatives, however, seemed very few. There where certainly a number of veterinarian surgeries in my neighbourhood; and I knew from childhood experience that people often took sick or unwanted animals there to be quietly put down. But I could not very well walk through the vet's front door and make a discreet enquiry about purchasing a dead black cat. I would immediately be thought of as a weirdo. The police might even be called and a confession forced from my throat. Then I would be in even more trouble than I am now. The advice from M. on this matter was unambiguous: seeking assistance from the police would result in a tragic loss of life. Mine.

You are probably thinking that I *am* some sort of weirdo, or perhaps that I am completely insane with my talk of strange internet sites that come and go, dead cats and fresh graves, and my inability to kill spiders, let alone cats. I can assure you that I was simply a desperate man who needs a very large sum of money in a very short space of time. You might think I have a gambling habit; that I've invested in shonky real estate deals on the Gold Coast; that I've been leading a lascivious life, squandering money on women, booze, and illicit drugs. You might also think that I had already borrowed too heavily from my friends and had now stooped to borrowing money from people who became dangerous enemies when they found I could not pay it back quickly enough. And you would be right to think such things, because, alas, it is all true. But reforming my behaviour was not my immediate concern; obtaining a large sum of money was. And there is only one being I know of who will happily provide that to me in a short space of time.

You might say: why not do what many other desperate men have done? Why all this nonsense talk of dead cats and graves, when you could simply rob a bank, a corner shop or a petrol station? But remember, flawed though I am, I am a pacifist who would be totally incapable of waving a gun about, threatening to shoot people's heads off if they did not hand over the money. No, any attempt along those lines would immediately be seen for the charade it was; and, no doubt, those I threatened would fall to the floor — not from fear — but from the laughter rumbling in their bellies. Besides, did I tell you I have an aversion to guns?

No, I have thought about this in a very rational manner and decided the irrational was my only option. That is, I would summon the Devil and seek his assistance. In this modern age, he is only a phone call away — provided, of course, you undertake the necessary ritual which alerts the evil gent to your presence. So a dead black cat was definitely called for.

Unfortunately, the internet offered no further assistance. I learnt there had been a famous horror movie called *The Black Cat* starring Boris Karloff and Bella Lugosi. I learnt that black cats were associated with evil in Babylonian and Hebrew mythologies. Also, black cats in Finland were thought to carry the souls of the dead to the other world, and during the Inquisition many a black cat was burnt at the stake. I even came across a pop-up advertisement enticing me to search for dead black cats currently on offer at eBay. Not surprisingly none were available; but I was advised to check again in a few days, obviously when the dead black cat market would be more buoyant. It seemed really that I had no choice but to trust to pure luck.

I took to driving the streets late at night, examining the road-kill by the side of the road. It seemed, however, that black cats were somewhat smarter than other cats at crossing roads. Dead tabbies there were aplenty and a surprising number of pedigree breeds, proving wrong it seemed the pretentious notion that pedigree cats were somehow more intelligent than your average moggy. Then on the sixth night, I believed I'd found what I was looking for: a poor dark bundle lying in the gutter in the shadow of a tree. Pulling on a pair of rubber gloves, I stepped from the car, glanced up and down the silent street, removed a sack from the boot, and deftly placed the cat inside. It was only upon returning home that I found the cat

NOT ANOTHER BLACK CAT STORY

wasn't black. It was instead a very dark grey that had easily been mistaken for black as it lay in the shadows. I placed the cat in the fridge while I thought what to do next.

At first, I was mortified. You may imagine my concern. It seemed right then that this had been my last chance and tomorrow morning I would need to ring M. and confess I had no money. I even thought of jumping in the car and driving away as fast as I could. It would give me a few days, perhaps even weeks, maybe a month, if I was lucky, but M. was the sort of person who had connections everywhere. It would be only a matter of time before he tracked me down. Then, all of a sudden, a clever idea, an epiphany of pure genius, struck me. You cannot deny that I had made progress. Before I had been catless, now at least I had a dead cat in the fridge. It was not quite the right colour, that was true; but my ex-wife, a natural brunette, managed successfully to spend her adult life as a blonde. I found my spirits rising and knew, with conviction, I was not far from my goal.

The following morning, I placed the dead cat in the bathtub and unwrapped my purchase from the local pharmacy. On the box there was a picture of a beautiful young woman with a dazzling smile and lustrous dark hair. Her particular shade of hair colouring, the writing on the box told me, was Midnight Black. I read the instructions carefully. The first step was to "wet hair thoroughly." I ran the shower and gently rolled the poor stiff moggy beneath it until its fur was well-soaked. It was surprising how skinny the cat was when wet. It was a slight little creature that obviously hadn't been well-fed by its owner. Next I massaged the dye into its fur, making sure it got into all the nooks and crannies, which wasn't easy as rigor mortis had set in and it was hard to get the dye up between its legs and into the furry little arm pits. But after ten or so minutes, I was indeed satisfied that my grey cat was well and truly covered in black. I left him for half an hour to allow the dye to take, then ran the shower again and gave him a good rinsing. From the bathroom cupboard, I took a big fluffy towel and dried him all over. Truth be known, I was growing quite fond of the cat; and, even though he was dead, I felt an almost fatherly affection as I played the blow dryer up and down his body, paying particular attention to drying inside his leathery ears.

I was most pleased with the result. The sheen I'd managed to achieve from careful application of the dye was wondrous to behold. The manufacturers had certainly been true to their words; the cat was a now a beautiful midnight black. If anything the lustre of its coat was greater even than the hair of the young woman used to advertise the product. Yes, I had my black cat and soon my ordeal would be over. I decided then that Midnight would be a suitable name for him.

THAT NIGHT, shortly before midnight, with my head-stones of Toowong cemetery. I was more than a little nervous, even if only at the thought of being in a cemetery so late at night. Who knew what dangers might be lurking there? Anything from drunken young men to the ghosts of psychotic killers was possible in a place such as this. But I steadied my fears by focussing on the task at hand. I had thought, as I drove to the cemetery, that it might not be as easy to find a freshly dug grave as I'd imagined. After all, Toowong cemetery is a big place, and I'd never had occasion to visit it previously. My anxiety in this regard, however, was soon allayed. After ten minutes, I came across a newer area of the cemetery where recent burials had taken place and was astonished to find there were a great many graves to choose from. On reflection, this should have been expected. It had been a long hot summer, and many of the older folks had taken the opportunity of the heat to breathe their last.

I stopped at the first fresh grave I came too, placed the sack on the ground, and ran my fingers through the soil. Finding it still moist, as opposed to crusty and dry, I decided the burial must have taken place that afternoon. This would do splendidly, I thought. I checked my mobile, as I had many times already that evening, to ensure it was fully charged and not about to die on me at the critical moment. Satisfied, I returned to the bag and withdrew Midnight from it. Firstly, I dragged him lengthwise from the head to the foot of the grave, then diagonally from left to right, then from right to left. As per the instructions, I placed Midnight at the point where all the lines intersected.

Cautiously, I stepped back from the grave and looked around me. How dark it seemed now and the breeze so chill, even though the air had been so warm earlier. I was overcome with a sudden sense of foolishness. A grown man performing some silly ritual at midnight in the cemetery with a dead cat he'd spent the morning dying black? Ridiculous! Pathetic! Even though I had denied it before, it seemed self-evident now that I was truly mad; and all of the stress of the last few months of my life had tipped me over the edge without my realising it. I bent down, meaning to return Midnight to the sack, to head back to the car, to give up on my fool's errand; but as I touched his body I felt a vibration running through it. Impossible, I thought, but as I began to stroke his fur, the vibration grew louder. There was no mistaking it. Midnight was purring.

The phone rang! Midnight and I almost jumped out of our skins. I pulled the mobile from my belt, pressed its answer button. "Yes," I said nervously.

"What do you think you're doing?" a thick voice asked brusquely.

"Is this . . . ?"

"Of course, it is!"

"Money," I said. "I need lots of money and I need it really soon."

"No."

I stared at the phone in disbelief. Who had ever heard of such a thing? The devil didn't wish to make a deal. Midnight had now fully recovered his senses. He was purring loudly and rubbing against my legs. I put the phone back up to my ear.

"This is the Devil, isn't it?" I asked.

"Yes," a weary voice said.

by Geoffrey Maloney   15

"And you do do deals?"

I imagined I heard somebody rapping their fingernails loudly and irritably on a heavy wooden table.

"The cat is grey," the Devil said. "The instructions were very specific on that point, were they not?"

"Yes. Yes, they were," I said, trying to sound as agreeable as possible.

"And you are offering me a grey cat?" the Devil said. "Is that what you are doing?"

"You should see him," I said. "He's a beautiful black cat. Why, I have never seen a cat as beautiful and black as he is. He is simply a marvellous black. Blacker than any cat could naturally be. Sometimes modern technology can really improve on nature."

I bent down and patted Midnight on top of the head. He rubbed his nose against my fingers. Through the phone I heard a sharp intake of breath. I thought the connection was about to go dead, but it didn't. Half a minute went by.

"I went to a lot of trouble dyeing him the right colour," I said. "I mean, people who just offer up naturally black cats don't go to the trouble I did."

"I like black cats," the Devil said.

"He really is very black," I said. "There was nothing on the website that specified he had to be *naturally* black."

There was a long sigh. "There is another problem," the Devil said. "You didn't kill him."

"He was dead. Most definitely. I know he's alive now — I guess you had something to do with that, a sign of your powers, and wondrous they are indeed."

"Yes, yes, yes, but *you* didn't kill him. You are supposed to be making a black cat sacrifice to the Devil. You know what a sacrifice is, don't you?"

"Um, yes. Yes, I think I do."

"So instead we have grey cat killed by a car? How do you think that makes me feel?"

"I can understand that you might be a little unhappy," I said, "but I have really been trying my best. The instructions said he had to be dead. And he was dead when I brought him here. The instructions didn't mention anything about a sacrifice."

Another long sigh from the phone. Of course, I should not be arguing with the Devil, I thought; but really if the instructions weren't correct what was I expected to do? If I had known I was supposed to actually kill a cat, I would have never thought of this solution in the first place. Besides, there were certain ethical considerations to be taken into account, even in dealing with the Devil. Honesty was paramount. I had followed the instructions as carefully as I could. Surely, even the Devil must see that.

"Wait!" came the Devil's voice. He sounded very angry. I could hear fingers tapping on a keyboard, and then a voice roared out as if from the very depths of Hell itself. My body shook all over with the force of the sound. I waited for fire and brimstone to rise up and engulf me, but then a different voice came on the line.

"Hello. Thank you for waiting. Your patience is appreciated while we endeavour to rectify the problems you have been experiencing."

"This is not the Devil, is it?"

"I'm one of the demon helpers. Now what was it you wanted?"

"To sort out the problem about the sacrifice, so I can sell my soul, get some money and save my life."

"All sorted," the demon helper chirped.

"I don't understand," I said.

"You offered one grey, road-kill cat; and — under the circumstances — it has been agreed that is acceptable. The website has been updated so that in future it will be abundantly clear to *others* that a naturally black cat is to be sacrificed."

"The money?" I asked hesitantly.

"I've updated your bank account even as we speak. I am sure that you will find the amount deposited more than sufficient for your purposes."

It was in that moment, I felt most chilled and fearful. My offer had been accepted! The transaction had been completed! The money was in my bank account! My soul was doomed to Hell!

"Is there anything else we can help you with?" the demon helper asked.

"My soul . . ." I whispered.

"Oh, yes, your soul. The Devil has decided to waive that particular condition. Frankly, between you and me, the Devil is most unhappy. He would prefer never to see or hear from you again. *You* made him feel fallible. He likes to have everything just so perfect all of the time and, as you have rightly, but annoyingly, pointed out, the website contained errors. There will be Hell to pay, I can assure you. Goodnight."

And with that the circuit went dead. I bent down to pick up Midnight. He cuddled into my arms, all soft and purring. It was only then I remembered I'd read on the internet that in some cultures black cats are actually lucky. I wondered how long his dye job would last.   ☙

Geoffrey Maloney lives in Brisbane, Australia with his wife, Diana, his three daughters and their three cats. Geoffrey's recent stories have appeared in the anthologies, When Graveyards Yawn *from Crowswing Books,* Agog Ripping Reads *from Agog Press, and* Fantastic Wonder Stories *from Ticonderoga. A largely retrospective collection of Geoffrey's short fiction,* Tales from the Crypto-System *is available from Prime Books.*

SCOUT

by Mary A. Turzillo

S*PRING EQUINOX. Whirring sound. Flashing lights. Whoosh of advanced propulsion system.*
"Mao! Mao! Mao! Mao! Mao! Mao! Mao!"
Door opens.
"Scat! Get away from here! Go home!"
"Mao!"

Fifteen minutes elapse.
"Mao! Mao! Mao! Mao! Mao! Mao! Mao! Mao! Mao! Mao-ao-ao-ao!"
"I *told* you, scat! Nothing for you here! *Go home!*"
"Mao! Mao!"
"Go chase some mice. Or birds. I hate birds."
"Maomaomaomao-ao-ao-ao!"
Splash. "There! Does that convince you? Now if I can just get back to sleep."

Six hours elapse.
"What? You still here? Somebody dropped you, right? Threw you out of a car? Do you have a collar?"
"Yooooow! Sssssssss! Raaaaawooo!
"Ow! Forget it. Just be gone when I get home from work."

"Prrt."

Nine hours elapse. Car pulls up, door slams. Foot-steps.
"Gone. Thank God. I was scared somebody took me for the cat lady over on Prospect."

Six hours elapse. Door opens.
"Mao?"
"Go away! I'm calling the Animal Warden and that's it. Hear me? Smoked kitty. Nice cyanide gas. Get! Scat!"
"Mao?"
"What are you doing? That has maggots on it. You can't eat that!"
"Prrrrrr."
"You're eating maggoty ham, and purring? That's disgusting!"
"Prrrrrrrrrrr."
"How could anything get hungry enough to eat rot-ten meat? Wait a minute."
Door closes, opens again.
"Here, here's the rest of my chicken wings. Hope you like garlic honey sauce. They're cold, anyway."
"Purrrrrrrrrrrrrrrrrrr."
"Get away from my legs! I hate that. Didn't I tell you I hate cats?"

Door slams. Eight hours elapse.
"Thank God it's gone. Found some other sucker."
Car door slams. Car starts, zooms away.

Three days elapse.
"Mao, mao, mao, mao, mao, mao, mao."
"You again? I don't have any more chicken wings. And I don't believe you if you say you're lost, because you left here Friday and then came back."
"Prrt?"
"Let me look at your collar. I bet some nice little stu-pid girl is just weeping her eyes out over you. Woosy woosy woosy woosy."
A brief chase.

"MAO!"

"Okay, so you have a collar, but no name on it. Real stupid little girl. She deserves to lose a prize flea-bag like you."

"Prrt."

"At least you didn't scratch me again."

Six hours elapse. Dusk gives way to nightfall. The air chills.

"Mao? Mao? Mao? Mao? Mao? Mao? Mao? MAO? MAO? MAOMAOMAOMAO?"

A window opens.

"Shut up down there! Remember what I did the last time you woke me up?"

Footsteps on stairs. Door opens.

"MAOMAOMAOMAOMAOMAOMAOMAO!"

"Let me guess. You're cold, right? If I give you something to sleep on, you'll get cat hair all over it. And fleas. And worms. I bet you have worms, eating garbage like that."

Door closes. Footsteps, sounds of rummaging. A piece of torn, dirty carpeting falls out of an upper window, **THUMPS** *on the ground, raises billows of dust.*

"Mao!"

Silence.

Seven hours elapse.

Door opens. "Where are you? Did you spend the night under the rug? Great, now what do I do with this piece of shit? I suppose I have to leave it, in case it's cold again tonight. A decorator touch for my entry."

Car door opens, closes, car speeds away.

Nine hours elapse.

"Here. For your majesty. It was cheap, and it looks better than that rug."

"Mao. Prrt."

"That's right. Show some gratitude, you little rat. You look like a rat, did you know that? You aren't much bigger than a rat. Well, hey, that's what eating maggoty garbage does for you. Not exactly the breakfast of champions. I suppose if I give you a little milk you'll think you can move in here, right? So I won't."

"Mao?"

"Not a chance. Go find your supper somewhere else."

"Mao? Mao?"

"And stop rubbing cat hair all over my pants!"

Door closes. Fifteen minutes elapse.

"Here! Will that shut you up?"

"Prrrrrrrrrrrrr. Slup. Slup. Slup. Prrrrrrr. Slup slup slup slup slup slup slup."

"That's the last you get out of me. I probably don't have enough left for my cereal in the morning."

Twenty-four hours elapse.

"Okay, one more time. But I looked up the Animal Shelter on the web. It says they let you stay five days, and then it's curtains for kitty cat. Okay? So I think you should move on."

Four hours elapse.

"Mao! Mao! Mao! Mao!"

"Look I don't have any chicken wings. How about some — french toast? Look, it's good, it's only been in the garbage since yesterday. Eat it. Eat it, you flea bag! It was good enough for me. Are you saying it's not good enough for you? Here, I'll butter it for you. Oh, you like that. Lick the butter off, huh?"

"Mao."

"No! I will not put more butter on it! Eat the whole thing, bread and all."

Twenty-four hours elapse.

"Mao! Mao! Mao! Mao!"

"Why are you still crying? Didn't you want the french toast? Yich! It's got flies on it."

"Waka."

"Waka? What does that mean? Cats don't say 'waka.' I'm not going to feed you if you don't speak proper English."

"Prrt."

"Wait a minute."

Car door slams. Car takes off.

Twenty minutes elapse. Car pulls up. Car door slams.

"Okay, you win. Cat food. This is probably a big mistake, but I'm not going out and buying you chicken wings."

Twelve hours elapse.

"Mao! Mao! Mao! Mao!"

Footsteps stumble down stairs. Door opens.

"At three A.M. you think I'm going to feed you? Oh. Your water overturned on the cat bed. Shit. Here. Here's an old sweatshirt."

"Prrt."

Four hours elapse.

"Here. You didn't ask for it, but I suppose you will. Here's your damn cat food. It stinks. I hope you love it."

"Mao."

"Is that your name, cat? Mao? Like Mao Tse Tung? You don't look Chinese to me." *[Subject kritches cat behind ears.]* "You look — hungry. You're kind of silky —"

A succession of days in which cat food appears in margarine tub. Spring advances. Warm weather. Cat eats food. Subject puts out more cat food.

"Pretty eyes. You might clean up nice. I'd let you in the house, but you'd bring in fleas. Let me think about this."

Subject switches to more expensive brand of cat food.

"You don't want to come in? Last chance."

*A*utumnal *equinox. Whirring sound. Flashing lights. Whoosh of advanced propulsion system.*

"Hey, cat! Cat! You didn't eat your food. I'm not going to buy any more unless you eat this. Hey, cat! Hey, Mao! Sneaky-paws! Where are you?"

by Mary A. Turzillo   23

Door left hopefully ajar.

Twelve hours elapse.
"Where are you? Pretty kitty! Mao!"

Another twelve hours.
"Where the Hell are you? Mao! Mao! Maaa-oh! Mao! Mao! Mao! Mao!"   🐾

Mary Turzillo's "Mars Is No Place for Children" won the 1999 Nebula for novelette. Her novel, An Old-Fashioned Martian Girl, *was serialized in* Analog, *and her poetry volume,* Your Cat Is a Space Alien, *will appear later this year. She lives with award-winning science-fiction author Geoff Landis and two cats, Lurker and Sam. The cats know many secrets, but they're not talking.*

AMERICAN CURLS

by Nancy Springer

THE MINUTE Cindy pulled into Samantha's driveway, she knew something was badly wrong. Both house and cattery doors stood wide open to six inches of February snow, and Samantha would never let that happen. Good grief, the kitties might catch pneumonia and die. Something must have happened to Sam, and there were no neighbors around to help, because an animal shelter always had to be way out in the country. But what could be the matter? Had Samantha fallen and hit her head, maybe?

Heaving herself out of her ancient Pinto, Cindy tightened her scarf around her thinning mousy hair, hustling toward Samantha's rancher at the fastest gait her plus-sized body would allow. Footprints riddled the snow, from volunteers and adoption seekers coming and going all day. But among them Cindy saw myriad little pawprints. Dear lord, every kitty in the place must have gotten out. They would freeze and starve and die. Even before she reached the house door and lunged inside, Cindy felt herself starting to cry.

But she stopped crying the instant she saw Samantha lying face down on the carpet, her caramel-colored spiral curls soaked red with blood. This was a matter too serious for crying. She knelt by Samatha's side, calling "Sam! Sam? Are you all right?"

Silence, except for pathetic meows from several directions. Some of the cats had stayed inside, evidently.

Cindy knew herself to be an idiot. Any fool could see Sam was not all right. With one chubby hand Cindy fumbled at the side of Sam's neck.

Yes, there was a pulse, but barely. Yes, Sam was taking a shallow breath now and then.

Cindy staggered up, yanked an afghan laden with much cat hair off the sofa and blanketed Sam. She called 911. Then she called Devon, who was the volunteer at the head of the emergency phone chain. Not that Devon was good for much except wielding her cell phone. Devon liked to brush the kitties, not clean up after them, and she never set foot in the shelter without wearing rubber gloves to protect her French-tip manicure. But she was efficient in her country-club way, didn't waste time being shocked, just said she'd call out the troops. After Cindy hung up, she checked Sam again — still unconscious, but breathing — then headed through the connecting door from the house into the cattery.

Six or seven cats flowed out of boxes and rubbed her ankles, a swirl of black, white, orange. Cindy felt her eyes fill with tears at the sight of them. Standing at the wide-open door, she called into the wind, "Here, kitty kitty kitty!"

But no kitties appeared. And oh, Lord, the box in the corner was empty. Where were the mamma cat and her litter? Following the feline mother's instinct to hide her young, Queenie had taken her weanling kittens out in the freezing cold. And already the day was darkening toward nightfall.

Cindy began to weep in earnest. Okay, Sam had fallen and hit her head on something. But who had let all the cats out? And why?

"SHE KEEPS MOST of them in the house," Cindy explained to the detectives.

Other volunteers wandered the night with flashlights, calling, peering into shrubbery, while Cindy cleaned up the mess in the cattery. "This room is just for the ones that don't use a litter box." Ferals, mostly, and the poor declaws. Didn't want to dig with their mutilated front paws. Several of them crowded Cindy's ankles, wailing like banshees. Cats were cats, even when they were designer kitties, purebred Himalayans and Cymrics and Russian Blues and Burmillas.

The cats lamented, and the detectives stood watching, but Cindy worked feverishly, gathering the dirty bedding, filling food and water bowls, then down on her knees scraping poop from the linoleum,. Shock wouldn't let her sit still. The cops said Samantha hadn't hit her head. They said somebody had hit it for her. With Sam's favorite cat figurine, the stylized teakwood Siamese, which might have doubled as a bowling pin. The hospital said Sam was in stable condition, but what if she didn't get well? What would happen to the kitties? What would happen to them now, poor babies lost in the cold?

"How many cats did she have?" a detective demanded.

"Ninety some."

"Good Lord."

"You see it all the time," said the other one, who was shorter and stockier. "Little old lady with too many cats."

"Whacked on the head?"

"Okay, so this one's a little old lesbian. Running a cathouse."

Cindy felt every overweight muscle tense. Samantha was not little, and not much older than 50, and as for her being a lesbian, so what? Sam ran a cat shelter, for mercy's sake, fully accredited, with records, volunteers, adoptions . . . these cops were jerks.

Cindy slammed her poop scraper into the sink and grabbed the scrub bucket.

"You'd know," the taller detective called to Cindy. "Who was her lover?"

Filling the bucket, Cindy just stared at him. She

knew nothing of Sam's personal life and didn't care to.

"Okay," he tried again, "did she have a live-in?"

"Nobody else lived here."

"Any frequent visitors?"

Cindy stared again, wishing she could do it more like a dragon and less like a cow. Luckily, just then one of the volunteers, the retarded girl, came in roaring softly to herself. Apparently this made the detectives uncomfortable. They retreated, ambling back into Sam's house. There wasn't much detecting for them to do, anyway. Sam would tell them when she woke up who had hit her.

The retarded girl set down an armload of snow-powdered cats. Cindy plopped herself on the floor, gathering kitties onto her lap to warm them and comfort them. And herself.

From time to time other volunteers tramped in, almost all middle-aged women like Cindy. Stamping and sniffling, they talked to the cats in their arms. "Watcha thing you're doing out there? Doncha know how cold it is?" Only one of them was a man, an odd, silent young fellow who said nothing as he turned his cats over to Cindy.

"It looks like every volunteer on the list came running," Cindy blurted at him just because she was uncomfortable with his silence.

He nodded, but didn't say a word as he headed back outside.

"I lied," Cindy told the kitties purring in her arms, nestled against her ample chest. "Devon's not here." Which was not surprising. Devon was a fair-weather volunteer. Didn't like to take her brand-new Beemer convertible out of the garage in anything less.

Another middle-aged woman stumbled in from the snowy night with a cat under each arm. "Padiddle and Rapunzel," she announced, setting down a one-eyed feral and a yellow longhair. "Has anyone found Queenie and the kittens?"

"No! Where in the world did she get to?" How far could the little gray tabby have gone with a litter of six? Cindy bit her lip. "I can't understand it."

* * *

MUCH LATER, Cindy got home — her home for the time being, anyway. A rather impressive Tudor in the best old neighborhood. Mrs. Heckmaster was sitting in the front room working on one of those memory books with the fancy pages and the stickers and lettering from the craft store. "My goodness," she said, glancing up as Cindy stamped snow off her feet in the entryway, "what's the matter, dear? You look like you need a cookie."

Mrs. Heckmaster was a little old lady with blue poodle curls, and Cindy did not like her. But she didn't need to like her, just keep an eye on her and run errands for her. Living with Mrs. Heckmaster earned Cindy her room and board while freeing Mrs. Heckmaster's family, which happened to consist of Devon, the fair-weather volunteer from the shelter. Devon Heckmaster, back to her maiden name and getting richer by the day off alimony, whereas Cindy felt herself getting poorer. When Mrs. Heckmaster graduated to a nursing home or croaked, Cindy would have to find some other person to live with as a nanny or a pet sitter or a caregiver.

Forty-six years old and homeless. But in Cindy's experience, it was people like her, the ones with the least, who did the most for animals. Well, with the exception of Devon . . . but Cindy volunteered for the SPCA, the horse sanctuary, the Dalmatian rescue and the Humane Action League, and she knew Devon was an anomaly. She knew of no other rich country clubbers who tried to help animals. Just ordinary folks. Like Samantha.

"It's Sam," Cindy told Mrs. Heckmaster. "Somebody hit her and let all the cats out."

"What? What are you talking about?" Mrs. Heckmaster leaned forward, predatory, an old vulture feeding on other people's excitement. But Cindy so badly needed to talk that she stuffed her butt into one of Mrs. Heckmaster's armchairs and told her all about it.

"We got most of the cats back inside by the time I left," she concluded, "but there's a few ferals still missing. And the one with kittens."

"I thought they spaded all those useless cats."

Spayed, Cindy thought. *Or neutered.* "They do. But Queenie was knocked up when she came." Yet another dumped pet. People like Mrs. Heckmaster thought they should be killed. They didn't understand.

"And the doctors think that sentimental fool Samantha is going to be all right?"

"That's what I heard." According to one of the volunteers, the doctors were keeping Samantha in a coma until her brain swelling went down.

Mrs. Heckmaster returned her attention to the memory book she was working on, a gift for her daughter, featuring news clippings about Devon's honors at various cat shows.

Devon was a cat fancier who raised American Curls, which was a weird new breed of cats with the ears bent over backwards. Cindy vaguely remembered hearing Devon talk about how the breed started with a mutation, like all those woolly Rex cats and those ugly hairless Sphinx ones and some others that Cindy couldn't remember. But Devon knew all about them. Which kind of explained her involvement in the cat rescue . . . no, it didn't. None of the other cat fanciers seemed to give a doo-diddle-dah about the strays Samantha took in.

"Do they know who hurt her?" Mrs. Heckmaster asked.

Cindy shook her head, silent, thinking about the retarded girl; could she have hit Samantha, maybe not understanding the consequences? Or what about that one male volunteer, so silent, so expressionless?

"I bet it's got something to do with her being light in her loafers," said Mrs. Heckmaster with relish.

Good lord, the old biddy reasoned just like the cops. Cindy got up to fetch Mrs. Heckmaster's bedtime meds, and as soon as her back was turned, she rolled her eyes.

TEN MINUTES before visiting hours the next day, Cindy lumbered into the hospital Ladies' Auxiliary Gift Shop.

"Why, hello, Cindy," said a familiar voice. "Have you come to see Samantha?"

Cindy blinked at Devon, who was speaking to her from behind the counter. Devon, with sleek blonde hair that had never been flattened by a scarf, every curl in place. Devon, so slim she made Cindy feel like a garbage can on feet. Devon, in a sage green wool dress so simple it must have cost five times what Cindy made in a week.

Cindy blurted, "I didn't know you worked here!"

"I volunteer here. I like to volunteer," said Devon with a little too much emphasis.

"Maybe you've heard, how's Samantha doing?"

"They say she's stable." Whatever that meant. "Did you want something to take to her?"

Cindy looked around the shop at pretty, useless stuff that made her yearn to have money: silk pansies in hand-painted country flowerpots, votive candles in cut-glass holders, miniature stuffed animals, winsome crockery kittens and puppies holding "Get Well" signs. Stalling for time, she asked, "Is she still in the coma, or did she wake up?"

"I wouldn't know. I haven't been to see her yet."

"Devon," called a woman from the shop's back room, phone in hand, "I've got a delivery order, huggy bear with daisies to room 402."

"I'll take it up in a minute."

Cindy wanted to get Sam a get-well kitten, but they were too expensive. She settled for a pansy pot ("Pansies Are For Thoughts") and headed off to find Samantha.

Eventually she located the room on a busy hallway with nurses rushing up and down. Sam's door was closed, which might mean the doctor was in there, or maybe they were giving her a bath. Cindy waited a while, but nobody came out. She knocked. Got no answer. She hesitated, then turned the knob and pushed the door open softly in case Sam was sleeping.

Afterward, she wondered whether she didn't have a premonition or something. But she didn't. Not an inkling.

She saw the pillow first. And fanning out from underneath it, caramel-colored spiral curls. Sam's hair.

Then she saw Sam's hand. Denim blue.

She screamed.

A nurse came running, pushed past her, made an unprofessional sound and rushed to lift the pillow from — from Samantha's face, very still, blue like Lake Placid. After that, Cindy didn't notice much. Nurses and doctors swept in and out, but Cindy stood where she was and stared at that blue face nested in spiral curls amid the bitterly bright room rife with get-well cards, bouquets of flowers, a knick-knack on the bedside table. . . .

Eventually, someone led her away to an office, where she sat. Time passed. She didn't notice.

"You again," said a male voice.

Cindy blinked and focused on the tall detective sitting across a desk from her.

"You found her," he said. "Again."

Cindy whispered, "She's dead."

"Yes, she is. Somebody finished the job. And I just have to wonder whether it's a coincidence, your being here."

Cindy didn't react. One good thing about being big was it helped her look stolid. She had a lot of inertia.

"Somebody smothered her and left the pillow in place," the detective said, watching her. "Might be some sort of kinky sex thing."

Cindy shook her head. Her thoughts had begun to move again, slowly but surely, like deep water. She blurted, "Did you get any prints off that cat statue they clubbed her with?"

The detective gave her a blank look. "I couldn't say."

This meant "No," Cindy reasoned, or he'd be inking her fingers this minute. "They wore gloves, right? Can you tell whether it was rubber gloves?"

He peered. "What makes you ask that?"

"One of those ceramic get-well kittens. In Sam's room. Who brought it up from the gift shop?"

BUT IT WAS ridiculous to suspect Devon, Cindy scolded herself as she drove toward the SPCA. What possible motive could Devon have to kill Samantha?

Still, Cindy felt agitated enough to double as a washing machine. With no idea what to think, she trudged into the SPCA for her weekly volunteer stint, wheeled the mop out and started to scrub, hoping the drudge work would calm her down.

Working her way between ranks of pens and cages, she patted the yipping dogs and mewling cats, but without feeling. Just reflex. When a little gray tabby rubbed its side against the woven wire, imploring, Cindy raised her hand automatically before several small fluffy movements caught her eye —

She squealed like an elephant. "Queenie!" she shrieked.

Queenie answered with a feline trill. It was the lost kittie, all right, complete with her litter of weanling kittens, their baby fur starting to grow out. "Queenie, you never told me your boyfriend was a longhair," Cindy cooed, because the kittens were turning into puffballs.

Footsteps pounded up the aisle. Cindy's screech had brought the manager running from the front desk.

"What's Queenie doing here?" Cindy demanded, turning on the woman as if it were her fault that Samantha's shelter was thirty miles away, in the next county, for God's sake.

"The little mama cat? Dumped," the woman said with fervid scorn. "That country clubber could certainly have afforded to make a donation, but noooo, dump and run."

Cindy felt something like a giant fist squeeze her chest, making it hard to breathe. She could force out only a couple of words. "Country clubber?"

"Yeah, yesterday morning, before we opened. I came in early, saw her hustling away. Blonde in a tennis outfit."

Cindy managed another few words. "Was she driving?"

"Sure. Shiny new car, red and white."

"A Beemer?" Devon's red convertible had a white ragtop.

"Heck, I don't know one car from another. Show me a dog, I know dogs."

It was ridiculous anyway. How would Devon have gotten hold of Queenie and the kittens? And what for? And why wouldn't she have said something? It was all nonsense. Cindy turned back to patting the little tabby and her adorable fluffy kittens. . . .

"So you know this mama cat?" the manager asked.

Intent on the kittens, Cindy didn't answer. One kitten, two, three, four, five. . . . "Where's the sixth one?" she demanded.

"She came with five. Phone's ringing." The woman ran to answer it.

Cindy closed her eyes a moment, visualizing Queenie's litter. Two tabbies, gray, like Queenie. Two spotted kittens. A black one with a white tuxedo bib. And the pure white one with the funny-looking fur.

She opened her eyes. It was the white kitten that was gone.

It had died in the cold, probably. Or Queenie had somehow lost track of it and left it behind. Or it could have been dropped out of the box. Any number of things could have happened to it, and there was no use wondering about it, was there?

AT NINE O'CLOCK that night, wearing a black top and black slacks, Cindy approached Devon's stately residence on foot, having parked her rusting Pinto on the next cul-de-sac over. Just as Mrs. Heckmaster lived in the best old section of town, Devon lived in the best new one, in a modernistic house. Getting in would be no problem. Mrs. Heckmaster had keys, and Cindy had appropriated them. On the keychain was a laminated card with the numbers for the security system. And this was Devon's night for modern dance class. Cindy foresaw no difficulties.

Just the same, she sweated as she unlocked a back door, silenced the alarm system, and slipped into the house through the garage.

She listened, and heard only a meow. She clicked on her flashlight and found herself in an immaculate back hallway the size of some people's apartments, with several cats padding to meet her. Why in the world — oh. Duh, they were American Curls, that was why their ears were inside out. Stupid looking, but they couldn't help it. Cindy whispered to them, "Where's the kitten, guys?"

She had tried to tell the detectives about her suspicions, but had succeeded only in making them look at her as if she had sprouted several extra heads. Jerks.

Silently, like the cats, Cindy padded to the first door and cautiously opened it. Just a storage room. Okay, onward to the next door. . . . Bingo. Cindy surveyed Devon's luxurious cattery, thickly carpeted, with scratching posts and climbing apparatus and a row of frilled, curtained cages for cat shows. From one of them sounded a meow as tiny as the piping of a nestling wren.

Cindy smiled, folded to her knees, opened the cage door and reached in past the porcelain litter pan to the miniature canopied bed. From atop a silk pillow she lifted the kitten.

"Well, hi, little fellow," she whispered, holding him in her lap as she shone the flashlight on him. He gazed back at her with unblinking blue eyes beneath white JonBenet curls — curls! Cindy gasped. All over the kitten's petite body, the new hair was growing out in long, soft curls worthy of Barbie at her prime, curls that made even Cindy's chapped hands itch for a comb and some ribbons and barrettes.

"Oh," she whispered, "you angel." With snowy little-girl curls, Shirley Temple curls, fashion-model, movie-star, all-American curls. "Pretty boy!"

Click went the light switch, the ceiling fixture blazed on, and Cindy jumped so hard she dropped her flashlight. There in the doorway stood Devon, exquisite in mauve silk pajamas, with quite a large carving knife in her hand.

Devon, with a look in her eyes fit to curl Cindy's very commonplace hair. Cindy knew she should be afraid, very afraid. But her wonder at the white kitten overrode her fear. She blurted, "He's a mutation, isn't he?"

Devon's lips twitched in a grimace too cold to be called a smile. "Imagine how much money people will pay," she said, "for a new breed of pretty kitty with long, silky, naturally curly hair."

An explosive mix of emotions lifted Cindy to her feet. "Is that what you killed Samantha for?" she cried.

"I never meant to hurt her! I just told her I wanted the kitten, and she got stupid about it."

A number of sleek cats with backward-tipped ears seated themselves on the cages as if on bleachers, watching. Devon advanced a step.

Keep her talking. Trying to think what to do, Cindy became polite and conversational. "Samantha knew this kitten was valuable?"

"No, she just wanted to keep him. The fool. I even offered to pay her for him." Devon's voice went squeaky shrill. "And she said no. After all the work I'd done for her stinking shelter! I lost my temper." Devon said this with a certain pride. "I thought I'd killed her."

Forget politeness. "Well, you did now, didn't you?"

Devon just showed her teeth. "What do you think?"

"I think you're a murderer." Holding the kitten gently even though her hands wanted to clench into fists, somehow Cindy found murder easier to accept than . . . "Did you have to put the cats out in the cold?"

"Don't be stupid. Of course I did. So no one would know I took one." Devon raised her knife. "Stick that kitten in his cage."

"No." As she said it, Cindy felt her sweat start to run cold.

"You always were a stupid lard-ass." Slowly, watching her fixedly, Devon advanced.

Devon in her mauve silk peejays, planning to spill her blood all over the thick cream-colored carpet. Sweating, Cindy blurted, "You're going to make an awful mess."

"So who's ever going to look?" Devon took another step toward her.

"I made substitutions in your mother's medicines." Cindy wished this were not a lie. "If I don't get back there before she goes to bed, you're going to have a very sick mother. She might even die."

Devon paused, considering, then paced forward again. "So let her die."

Cindy lifted the white kitten in both shaking hands. "If you take one more step, I'll wring his neck."

But Devon gave a cold bark of laughter. "Bull. You're an overstuffed cream puff."

One more step put her almost within arm's reach of Cindy.

"Here. Catch!" Cindy tossed the kitten at her. Devon squeaked, grabbing for the baby reflexively, and Cindy bent over and lunged to head-ram Devon just below the ribs with all the force of her way-too-many pounds.

She flattened Devon, fell on top of her, and lay there panting, mostly with relief that she did not feel any knife sticking into her. There it was, lying on the carpet several feet away. Cindy started to shake, but that was okay. She closed her eyes, taking time to recover, to think what to do next. Under her, enveloped by her, Devon struggled briefly, then apparently decided it was no use and lay still. In order to restrain Devon, all Cindy had to do was remain lying on top of her. Overweight had its advantages.

She lay catching her breath a few more minutes before something wet and raspy massaged her face. One of the cats was licking her . . . oh, God, where was the kitten? Was it all right?

Cindy opened her eyes, took a look around, and there was the white kitten, just fine, batting at the carving knife's shiny blade.

"Stop that. You'll hurt yourself," Cindy muttered, knowing she should get up and take possession of the knife. But she still felt shaky. That and inertia kept her where she was. Even the sound of running footsteps in the hallway didn't budge her.

A pair of battered brogans appeared in the doorway below rumpled khakis. Suddenly lighthearted, Cindy heaved herself up to stand facing the tall detective.

He waved her to one side. In his other hand he held his pistol at the ready. "Tailed you," he explained while never taking his eyes from Devon. "Heard most of it from outside the window." He ordered Devon, "Ms. Heckmaster, clasp your hands on top of your head!"

Devon did not respond, just lay still. Very, very still. Staring blankly at the ceiling.

Cindy started to shake again. "I knocked the breath out of her," she murmured, "then lay on top of her . . . oh, my God."

The white kitten bounded over to Devon and pounced on her trailing blonde hair. He clutched her golden locks in his tiny paws, then climbed her head to prance on her face. He batted at her motionless eyebrows, lost his balance, and sat his furry little butt on her nose. He piped a soprano meow. From atop Devon's corpse he gazed at the world he was born to conquer, his wide blue eyes haloed by angelic curls.

🐾

Nancy Springer is closing in on book publication number fifty and Social Security check number one at about the same time. After 46 years in Pennsylvania, she is both startled and pleased to find herself moving to the Florida panhandle, where she, her husband, three pets, and four airplanes will be living in a hangar at a small general-aviation airfield.

AMERICAN CURLS

THE CATS OF ULTHAR

by H.P. Lovecraft

IT IS SAID that in Ulthar, which lies beyond the river Skai, no man may kill a cat; and this I can verily believe as I gaze upon him who sitteth purring before the fire. For the cat is cryptic, and close to strange things which men cannot see. He is the soul of antique Aegyptus, and bearer of tales from forgotten cities in Meroë and Ophir. He is the kin of the jungle's lords, and heir to the secrets of hoary and sinister Africa. The Sphinx is his cousin, and he speaks her language; but he is more ancient than the Sphinx, and remembers that which she hath forgotten.

In Ulthar, before ever the burgesses forbade the killing of cats, there dwelt an old cotter and his wife who delighted to trap and slay the cats of their neighbors. Why they did this I know not; save that many hate the voice of the cat in the night, and take it ill that cats should run stealthily about yards and gardens at twilight. But whatever the reason, this old man and woman took pleasure in trapping and slaying every cat which came near to their hovel; and from some of the sounds heard after dark, many villagers fancied that the manner of slaying was exceedingly peculiar. But the villagers did not discuss such things with the old man and his wife; because of the habitual expression on the withered faces of the two, and because their cottage was so small and so darkly hidden under spreading oaks at the back of a neglected yard. In truth, much as the owners of cats hated these odd folk, they feared them more; and instead of berating them as brutal assassins, merely took care that no cherished pet or mouser should stray toward the remote hovel under the dark trees. When through some unavoidable oversight a cat was missed, and sounds heard after dark, the loser would lament impotently; or console himself by thanking Fate that it was not one of his children who had thus vanished. For the people of Ulthar were simple, and knew not whence it is all cats first came.

One day a caravan of strange wanderers from the South entered the narrow cobbled streets of Ulthar. Dark wanderers they were, and unlike the other roving folk who passed through the village twice every year. In the market-place they told fortunes for silver, and bought gay beads from the merchants. What was the land of these wanderers none could tell; but it was seen that they were given to strange prayers, and that they had painted on the sides of their wagons strange figures with human bodies and the heads of cats, hawks, rams, and lions. And the leader of the caravan wore a headdress with two horns and a curious disk betwixt the horns.

There was in this singular caravan a little boy with no father or mother, but only a tiny black kitten to cherish. The plague had not been kind to him, yet had left him this small furry thing to mitigate his sorrow; and when one is very young, one can find great relief in the lively antics of a black kitten.

So the boy whom the dark people called Menes smiled more often than he wept as he sat playing with his graceful kitten on the steps of an oddly painted wagon.

On the third morning of the wanderers' stay in Ulthar, Menes could not find his kitten; and as he sobbed aloud in the market-place certain villagers told him of the old man and his wife, and of sounds heard in the night. And when he heard these things his sobbing gave place to meditation, and finally to prayer. He stretched out his arms toward the sun and prayed in a tongue no villager could understand; though indeed the villagers did not try very hard to understand, since their attention was mostly taken up by the sky and by the odd shapes the clouds were assuming. It was very peculiar, but as the little boy uttered his petition there seemed to form overhead the shadowy, nebulous figures of exotic things; of hybrid creatures crowned with horn-flanked disks. Nature is full of such illusions to impress the imaginative.

That night the wanderers left Ulthar, and were never seen again. And the householders were troubled when they noticed that in all the village there was not a cat to be found. From each hearth, the familiar cat had vanished; cats large and small, black, grey, striped, yellow, and white. Old Kranon, the burgomaster, swore that the dark folk had taken the cats away in revenge for the killing of Menes's kitten; and cursed the caravan and the little boy. But Nith, the lean notary, declared that the old cotter and his wife were more likely persons to suspect; for their hatred of cats was notorious and increasingly bold. Still, no one durst complain to the sinister couple; even when little Atal, the innkeeper's son, vowed that he had at twilight seen all the cats of Ulthar in that accursed yard under the trees, pacing very slowly and solemnly in a circle around the cottage, two abreast, as if in performance of some unheard-of rite of beasts. The villagers did not know how much to believe from so small a boy; and though they feared that the evil pair had charmed the cats to their death, they preferred not to chide the old cotter till they met him outside his dark and repellent yard.

So Ulthar went to sleep in vain anger; and when the people awakened at dawn — behold! every cat was back at his accustomed hearth! Large and small, black, grey, striped, yellow, and white: none was missing. Very sleek and fat did the cats appear, and sonorous with purring content. The citizens talked with one another of the affair, and marveled not a little. Old Kranon again insisted that it was the dark folk who had taken them, since cats did not return alive from the cottage of the ancient man and his wife. But all agreed on one thing: that the refusal of all the cats to eat their portions of meat or to drink their saucers of milk was exceedingly curious. And for two whole days the sleek, lazy cats of Ulthar would touch no food, but only doze by the fire or in the sun.

It was fully a week before the villagers noticed that no lights were appearing at dusk in the windows of the cottage under the trees. Then the lean Nith remarked that no one had seen the old man or his wife since the night the cats were away. In another week the burgomaster decided to overcome his fears and call at the strangely silent dwelling as a matter of duty, though in so doing he was careful to take with him Shang the blacksmith and Thul the cutter of stone as witnesses. And when they had broken down the frail door they found only this: two cleanly picked human skeletons on the earthen floor, and a number of singular beetles crawling in the shadowy corners.

There was subsequently much talk among the burgesses of Ulthar. Zath, the coroner, disputed at length with Nith, the lean notary; and Kranon and Shang and Thul were overwhelmed with questions. Even little Atal, the innkeeper's son, was closely questioned and given a sweetmeat as reward. They talked of the old cotter and his wife, of the caravan of dark wanderers, of small Menes and his black kitten, of the prayer of Menes and of the sky during that prayer, of the doings of the cats on the night the caravan left, and of what was later found in the cottage under the dark trees in the repellent yard.

And in the end the burgesses passed that remarkable law which is told of by traders in Hatheg and discussed by travelers in Nir; namely, that in Ulthar no man may kill a cat.   🐾

H.P. Lovecraft (1890–1937) was not only the creator of the now world-famous Cthulhu Mythos, but a serious cat person, whose letters and essays repeatedly

THE CATS OF ULTHAR

celebrate the superiority of the aristocratic cat over the "peasant" dog. When he lived just beyond the outskirts of Brown University, he described the doings of the Kappa Alpha Tau fraternity, which met on a rooftop below his study window. His most felinophilic work other than the present story is "The Dream Quest of Unknown Kadath."

KREATIVITY FOR KATS

by Fritz Leiber

GUMMITCH PEERED thoughtfully at the molten silver image of the sun in his little water bowl on the floor inside the kitchen window. He knew from experience that it would make dark ghost-suns swim in front of his eyes for a few moments, and that was mildly interesting. Then he slowly thrust his head out over the water, careful not to ruffle its surface by rough breathing, and stared down at the mirror cat — the Gummitch Double — staring up at him. Gummitch had early discovered that water mirrors are very different from most glass mirrors. The scentless spirit world behind glass mirrors is an upright one sharing our gravity system, its floor a continuation of the floor in the so-called real world. But the world in a water mirror has reverse gravity. One looks down into it, but the spirit-doubles in it look *up* at one. In a way water mirrors are holes or pits in the world, leading down to a spirit infinity or ghostly nadir.

Gummitch had pondered as to whether, if he plunged into such a pit, he would be sustained by the spirit gravity or fall forever. (It may well be that speculations of this sort account for the caution about swimming, which is characteristic of most cats.)

There was at least one exception to the general rule. The looking glass on Kitty-Come-Here's dressing tables also opened into a spirit world of reverse gravity, as Gummitch had discovered when he happened to look into it during one of the regular visits he made to the dressing table top, to enjoy the delightful flowery and musky odors emanating from the fragile bottles nestled there.

But exceptions to general rules, as Gummitch knew well, are only doorways to further knowledge and finer classifications. The wind could not get into the spirit world below Kitty-Come-Here's looking glass, while one of the definitive characteristics of water mirrors is that movement can very easily enter the spirit world below them, rhythmically disturbing it throughout, producing the most surreal effects, and even reducing it to chaos. Such disturbances exist only in the spirit world and are in no way a mirroring of anything in the real world: Gummitch knew that his paw did not change when it flicked the surface of the water, although the image of his paw burst into a hundred flickering fragments. (Both cats and primitive men first deduced that the world in a water mirror is a spirit world because they saw that its inhabitants were easily blown apart by the wind and must therefore be highly tenuous, though capable of regeneration.)

Gummitch mildly enjoyed creating rhythmic disturbances in the spirit worlds below water mirrors. He wished there were some way to bring their excitement and weird beauty into the real world.

ON THIS SUNNY DAY when our story begins, the spirit world below the water mirror in his drinking bowl was particularly vivid and bright. Gummitch stared for a while longer at the Gummitch Double and then thrust down his tongue to quench his thirst. Curling swiftly upward, it conveyed a splash of water into his mouth and also flicked a single drop of water into the air before his nose. The sun struck the drop, and it flashed like a diamond. In fact, it seemed to Gummitch that for a moment he had juggled the sun on his tongue. He shook his head amazedly and touched the side of the bowl with his paw. The bowl was brimful and a few drops fell out; they also flashed like tiny suns as they fell. Gummitch had a fleeting vision, a momentary creative impulse, that was gone from his mind before he could seize it. He shook his head once more, backed away from the bowl, and then lay down with his head pillowed on his paws to contemplate the matter.

The room darkened as the sun went under a cloud, and the young golden dark-barred cat looked like a pool of sunlight left behind. Kitty-Come-Here had watched the whole performance from the door to the dining room and that evening she commented on it to Old Horsemeat.

"He backed away from the water as if it were poison," she said. "They have been putting more chlorine in it lately, you know, and maybe he can taste the fluorides they put in it for dental decay."

Old Horsemeat doubted that, but his wife went on, "I can't figure out where Gummitch does his drinking these days. There never seems to be any water gone from his bowl. And we haven't had any cut flowers. And none of the faucets drip."

"He probably does his drinking somewhere outside," Old Horsemeat guessed. "But he doesn't go outside very often these days,"

Kitty-Come-Here countered. "Scarface and the Mad Eunuch, you know. Besides, it hasn't rained for weeks. It's certainly a mystery to me where he gets his liquids. Boiling gets the chlorine out of water, doesn't it? I think I'll try him on some tomorrow."

"Maybe he's depressed," Old Horsemeat suggested. "That often leads to secret drinking."

This baroque witticism hit fairly close to the truth. Gummitch *was* depressed — had been depressed ever since he had lost his kittenish dreams of turning into a man, achieving spaceflight, learning and publishing all the secrets of the fourth dimension, and similar marvels. The black cloud of disillusionment at realiz-

KREATIVITY FOR KATS

ing he could only be a cat had lightened somewhat, but he was still feeling dull and unfulfilled.

Gummitch was at that difficult age of he-cats, between First Puberty, when the cat achieves essential maleness, and Second Puberty, when he gets broad-chested, jowly, and thick-ruffed, becoming a fully armed sexual competitor. In the ordinary course of things, he would have been spending much of his time exploring the outer world, detail-mapping the immediate vicinity, spying on other cats, making cautious approaches to unescorted females and in all ways comporting himself like a fledgling male. But this was prevented by the two burly toms who lived in the houses next door and who, far more interested in murder than the pursuit of mates, had entered into partnership with the sole object of bushwhacking-Gummitch. Gummitch's household had nicknamed them Scarface and the Mad Eunuch, the latter being one of those males whom "fixing" turns, not placid, but homicidally maniacal. Compared to these seasoned heavyweights, Gummitch was a welterweight at most. Scarface and the Mad Eunuch lay in wait for him by turns just beyond the kitchen door, so that his forays into the outside world were largely reduced to dashes for some hiding hole, followed by long, boring, but perilous sieges.

He often wished that Old Horsemeat's two older cats, Ashurbanipal and Cleopatra, hadn't gone to the country to live with Old Horsemeat's mother. They would have shown the evil bushwhackers a thing or two!

BECAUSE OF SCARFACE and the Mad Eunuch, Gummitch spent most of his time indoors. Since a cat is made for a half-and-half existence — half in the wild forest, half in the secure cave — he took to brooding quite morbidly. He thought over-much of ghost cats in the mirror world and of Skeleton Cat who starved to death in a locked closet and similar grisly legends. He immersed himself in racial memories, not so much of Ancient Egypt where cats were prized as

minions of the lovely cat-goddess Bast and ceremoni-
ously mummified at the end of tranquil lives, as of the
Middle Ages, when European mankind waged a geno-
cide war against felines as being the familiars of
witches. (He thought briefly of turning Kitty-Come-
Here into a witch, but his hypnotic staring and tenta-
tive ritualistic mewing only made her fidgety.) And he
devoted more and more time to devising dark versions
of the theory of transmigration, picturing cats as Silent Souls, Gagged People of Great Talent, and the
like. He had become too self-conscious to re-enter often the make-believe world of the kitten, yet his imagination remained as active as ever. It was a truly
frustrating predicament.

More and more often and for longer periods he re-
tired to meditate in a corrugated cardboard shoe-box,
open only at one end. The cramped quarters made it
easier for him to think. Old Horsemeat called it the
Cat Orgone Box after the famed Orgone Energy Accu-
mulators of the late, wildcat psychoanalyst Dr. Wil-
helm Reich.

If only, Gummitch thought, he could devise some
way of objectifying the intimations of beauty that flit-
ted through his darkly clouded mind! Now, on the evening of the sunny day when he had backed away from
his water bowl, he attacked the problem anew. He
knew he had been fleetingly on the verge of a great
idea, an idea involving water, light, and movement.
An idea he had unfortunately forgotten. He closed his
eyes and twitched his nose. *I must concentrate,* he
thought to himself, *concentrate . . .*

NEXT DAY, Kitty-Come-Here remembered her idea
about Gummitch's water. She boiled two cupfuls in a
spotless enamelware saucepan, letting it cool for half
an hour before using it to replace the seemingly offen-
sive water in the young cat's bowl. It was only then
she noticed that the bowl had been upset.

She casually assumed that big-footed OldHorse-
meat must have been responsible for the accident, or

possibly one of the two children — darting Sissy or blundering Baby. She wiped the bowl and filled it with the water she had dechlorinated.

"Come here, Kitty, come here," she called to Gummitch, who had been watching her actions attentively from the dining room door. The young cat stayed where he was. "Oh, well, if you want to be coy," she said, shrugging her shoulders.

There was a mystery about the spilled water. It had apparently disappeared entirely, though the day seemed hardly dry enough for total evaporation. Then she saw it standing in a puddle by the wall fully ten feet away from the bowl. She made a quick deduction and frowned a bit worriedly.

"I never realized the kitchen floor sloped *that* much," she told Old Horsemeat after dinner. "Maybe some beams need to be jacked up in the basement. I'd hate to think of collapsing into it while I cooked dinner."

"I'm sure this house finished all its settling thirty years ago," her husband assured her hurriedly. "That slope's always been there."

"Well, if you say so," Kitty-Come-Here allowed doubtfully.

Next day she found Gummitch's bowl upset again and the remains of the boiled water in a puddle across the room. As she mopped it up, she began to do some thinking without benefit of the Concentration Box.

THAT EVENING, after Old Horsemeat and Sissy had vehemently denied kicking into the water bowl or stepping on its edge, she voiced her conclusions. "I think *Gummitch* upsets it," she said. "He's rejecting it. It still doesn't taste right to him and he wants to show us."

"Maybe he only likes it after it's run across the floor and got seasoned with household dust and the corpses of germs," suggested Old Horsemeat, who believed most cats were bohemian types.

"I'll have you know I *scrub* that linoleum," Kitty-Come-Here asserted.

"Well, with detergent and scouring powder, then," Old Horsemeat amended resourcefully.

Kitty-Come-Here made a scornful noise. "I still want to know where he gets his liquids," she said. "He's been off milk for weeks, you know, and he only drinks a little broth when I give him that. Yet he doesn't seem dehydrated. It's a real mystery and —"

"Maybe he's built a still in the attic," Old Horsemeat interjected.

"— and I'm going to find the answers," Kitty-Come-Here concluded, ignoring the facetious interruption. "I'm going to find out *where* he gets the water he does drink and *why* he rejects the water I give him. This time I'm going to boil it and put in a pinch of salt. Just a pinch."

"You make animals sound more delicate about food and drink than humans," Old Horsemeat observed.

"They probably are," his wife countered. "For one thing, they don't smoke, or drink martinis. It's my firm belief that animals — cats, anyway — like good food just as much as we do. And the same sort of good food. They don't enjoy canned catfood any more than we would, though they *can* eat it. Just as we could, if we had to. I really don't think Gummitch would have such a passion for raw horsemeat except you started him on it so early."

"He probably thinks of it as steak tartare," Old Horsemeat said.

Next day Kitty-Come-Here found her salted offering upset just as the two previous bowls had been.

SUCH WERE the beginnings of the Great Spilled Water Mystery that preoccupied the human members of the Gummitch household for weeks. Not every day, but frequently, and sometimes two and three times a day, Gummitch's little bowl was upset. No one ever saw the young cat do it. But it was generally accepted that he was responsible, though for a time Old Horsemeat had theories that he did not voice involving Sissy and Baby.

Kitty-Come-Here brought Gummitch a firm-footed

rubber bowl for his water, though she hesitated over the purchase for some time, certain that he would be able to taste the rubber. This bowl was found upset just like his regular china one and like the tin one she briefly revived from his kitten days. All sorts of clues and possibly related circumstances were seized upon and dissected. For instance, after about a month of the mysterious spillings, Kitty-Come-Here announced, "I've been thinking back and as far as I can remember it never happens except on sunny days."

"Oh, Good Lord!" Old Horsemeat reacted. Meanwhile Kitty-Come-Here continued to try to concoct a kind of water that would be palatable to Gummitch. As she continued without success, her formulas became more fantastic. She quit boiling it for the most part but added a pinch of sugar, a spoonful of beer, a few flakes of oregano, a green leaf, a violet, a drop of iodine . . .

"No wonder he rejects the stuff," Old Horsemeat was tempted to say, but didn't.

Finally Kitty-Come-Here, inspired by the sight of a greenly glittering rack of it at the supermarket, purchased a half gallon of bottled water from a famous spring. She wondered why she hadn't thought of this step earlier — it certainly ought to take care of her haunting convictions about the unpalatableness of chlorine or fluorides. (She herself could distinctly taste the fluorides in the tap water, though she never mentioned this to Old Horsemeat.)

One other development during the Great Spilled Water Mystery was that Gummitch gradually emerged from depression and became quite gay. He took to dancing cat schottisches and gigues impromptu in the living room of an evening and so forgot his dignity as to battle joyously with the vacuum cleaner dragon when Old Horsemeat used one of the smaller attachments to curry him; the young cat clutched the hairy round brush to his stomach and madly clawed it as it *whuffled* menacingly. Even the afternoon he came home with a shoulder gashed by the Mad Eunuch he seemed strangely light-hearted and debonair.

by Fritz Leiber   51

THE MYSTERY was abruptly solved one sunny Sunday afternoon. Going into the bathroom in her stocking feet, Kitty-Come-Here saw Gummitch apparently trying to drown himself in the toilet. His hindquarters were on the seat but the rest of his body went down into the bowl. Coming closer, she saw that his forelegs were braced against the opposite side of the bowl, just above the water surface, while his head thrust down sharply between his shoulders. She could distinctly hear rhythmic lapping.

To tell the truth, Kitty-Come-Here was rather shocked. She had certain rather fixed ideas about the delicacy of cats. It speaks well for her progressive grounding that she did not shout at Gummitch but softly summoned her husband.

By the time Old Horsemeat arrived the young cat had refreshed himself and was coming out of his "well" with a sudden backward undulation. He passed them in the doorway with a single mew and upward look, and then made off for the kitchen.

The blue and white room was bright with sunlight. Outside the sky was blue and the leaves were rustling in a stiff breeze. Gummitch looked back once, as if to make sure his human congeners had followed, mewed again, and then advanced briskly toward his little bowl with the air of one who proposes to reveal all mysteries at once.

Kitty-Come-Here had almost outdone herself. She had for the first time poured him the bottled water, and she had floated a few rose petals on the surface.

Gummitch regarded them carefully, sniffed at them, and then proceeded to fish them out one by one and shake them off his paw. Old Horsemeat repressed the urge to say, "I told you so."

When the water surface was completely free and winking in the sunlight, Gummitch curved one paw under the side of the bowl and jerked.

Half the water spilled out, gathered itself, and then began to flow across the floor in little rushes, a silver ribbon sparkling with sunlight that divided and subdivided and reunited as it followed the slope. Gummitch crouched to one side, watching it intensely, following its progress inch by inch and foot by foot, almost pouncing on the little temporary pools that formed, but not quite touching them. Twice he mewed faintly in excitement.

"HE'S PLAYING with it," Old Horsemeat said incredulously.

"No," Kitty-Come-Here countered wide-eyed, "he's creating something. Silver mice. Water-snakes. Twinkling vines."

"Good Lord, you're right," Old Horsemeat agreed. "It's a new art form. Would you call it water painting? Or water sculpture? Somehow I think that's best. As if a sculptor made mobiles out of molten tin."

"It's gone so quickly, though," Kitty-Come-Here objected, a little sadly. "Art ought to last. Look, it's almost all flowed over to the wall now."

"Some of the best art forms are completely fugitive," Old Horsemeat argued. "What about improvisation in music and dancing? What about jam sessions and shadow figures on a wall? Gummitch can always do it again — in fact, he must have been doing it again and again last month. It's never exactly the same, like waves or fire. But it's beautiful."

"I suppose so," Kitty-Come-Here said. Then coming to herself, she continued, "But I don't think it can be healthy for him to go on drinking water out of the toilet. Really."

Old Horsemeat shrugged. He had an insight about the artistic temperament and the need to dig for inspiration into the smelly fundamentals of life, but it was difficult to express delicately.

Kitty-Come-Here sighed, as if bidding farewell to all her efforts with rose petals and crystalline bottled purity and vanilla extract and the soda water which had amazed Gummitch by faintly spitting and purring at him.

"Oh, well," she said, "I can scrub it out more often, I suppose."

Meanwhile, Gummitch had gone back to his bowl

and, using both paws, overset it completely. Now, with nose a-twitch, he once more pursued the silver streams alive with suns, refreshing his spirit with the sight of them. He was fretted by no problems about what he was doing. He had solved them all with one of his characteristically sharp distinctions: there was the *sacred* water, the sparklingly clear water to create with, and there was the water with character, the water to *drink*. ❖

Fritz Leiber (1910–1992) was best known for his Fafhrd and Gray Mouser series of sword-and-sorcery adventures, but he also wrote a broad range of fantastic fiction, including such classics as The Big Time *and* The Wanderer *(which features a memorable cat-woman alien). An entire volume of his cat fiction,* Gummitch and Friends, *was published by Donald M. Grant in 1992. This includes the Hugo-winning novella, "Ship of Shadows." Leiber ultimately collected just about every award the field has ever had to offer.*

KREATIVITY FOR KATS

NON-EXISTENT CATS

by Tony Richards

THIS, AS THE TITLE already tells you, is all about cats that aren't there. And by 'cats,' I mean the small domestic kind, not big lions and other stuff, or cool, jazz-type people.

Are you with me so far? Good.

Anyway, it started like this: The phone went, about nine in the morning. I was half way into my pants, the store opening at ten, and had to hop over to answer it. And when I pick it up I hear like, *"Lenn-iieee!"*

My name's Leonard Melnic, by the way. Just Len to my friends. My girlfriend's the only person that I let call me 'Lenny' since, like what, I'm still going to have people call me Lenny when I'm one hundred years old or something? I'm twenty four, and am into comic books and garage music and all kind of films, except sub-titled ones. I have this party trick where I play bongos and eat a whole Big Mac at the same time — *you* try it. Not so easy, huh? And I work at that big alternative bookstore on Union, Rolling Paper.

My girlfriend's Megan, and she's only — erm — eighteen, and a Goth. Which means she has long, very straight dark hair with purple streaks in it, and is into S&M clothes and imagery, though not the reality. We tried a spanking session once, at *her* insistence, and she didn't speak to me for practically a whole week.

So anyway, *"Lenn-iieee!"*

And it's Megan, which surprises me since she only works at the beauty parlour in the afternoon and is usually right out of it until at least ten thirty.

"Hey, what's up?"

"Get over here, *please!"*

"Are you all right?"

"Of course not! There's been a cat in my room! I got up to pee, and there were scratches on the furniture!"

So I look at my watch. Megan's is ten minutes away. The store? Twenty, in the other direction.

"Is it still there?"

"That's what I want you to find out!"

And then she starts making this whimpering noise that simply breaks my heart.

The strange thing about Megan, see, is that even though she's a Goth and into all kinds of witchy stuff like candles and amulets and Tolkein posters, she just can't stand cats. In the first place, they give her the creeps. And in the second, she's allergic to them.

I don't like them either. They're all sniffy, like some fox who won't give you the time of day. And they have this thing where they jump in your lap and you try to get them off, and they don't want to move and dig their claws in. Yow! But I'm not scared of them the way Megan is. So I get over there.

I go up the staircase to her third floor walk-up, and when I knock on the door I hear this thump, like someone jumping around. And the door comes open a few seconds later, and there's Megan standing there, looking cute in just her scanties, but looking pretty wide-eyed and scared with it.

"What was that noise?" I ask her.

"I was standing on the bed."

"I thought that was for mice? What, like a cat can't climb up on a bed?"

"Oh, shut up, stupid! Just get in here!" And she yanks me inside, strong despite the fact she's pretty tiny. *"Look* for the damn thing!"

So I begin The Great Cat Hunt. Megan hops back on the bed, teetering around and looking foxier than ever. And she keeps trying to direct me, going, "over there, look behind that," and such-like. But who's doing the work here, me or her?

All I find of interest, in the end, is a pile of old teen romance mags in the bottom of a closet, and a big purple vibrator that I've never seen before. And Megan jumps off the bed and snatches it out of my hand and puts it away at that point, so she's obviously calmed down a little.

"There's nothing here," I tell her, still smirking a bit about the vibrator and the way she's looking flushed. "It probably went out through the window."

"That's the crazy thing!" she wails now. "There weren't any windows open! How could the thing get in *or* out?"

So I ask her to show me the scratches. And there they are, clear as day, on two of the legs of her rickety dining table and one of the chairs. I bend down and inspect them carefully. And finally, I purse my lips.

"Hmm, it looks like a cat." I hope that my tone sounds impressive. "Do you think it could be Mr. Paws?"

But Megan sounds less than overwhelmed by my brilliant deduction.

Fortunately for her, there are no cats in her building since pets aren't allowed. But if you look out her kitchen window into the space out back, you can usually see a big fat tabby sitting on the first floor window ledge of the building behind this one. He belongs to an old lady, and is the laziest cat you've ever seen, only ever moving himself at meal-times. We looked out the window now, and there he was, a rotund ball of fur.

Mr. Paws couldn't climb onto a cinderblock, let alone up here.

So we're both pretty puzzled. I do my best to calm her down, which involves kidding her a lot and tickling her. And the fact that she's still in her underwear starts to get to both of us.

But I'm already late at the store. I swear it, man, this Protestant Work Ethic shit? It's gonna be the death of me.

NINE-THIRTY the next morning, the phone goes again.

"*Lenn-iiee!*"

And I think, *oh fuck.*

"My *curtains* are shredded! I think it's still hiding in here!"

But I know perfectly well it isn't. Megan's place isn't that big, and I searched every square inch of it. I remind her of that, getting rather annoyed while I do so.

"If I come round there, I'm going to be late again, and Chan'll have my guts!"

"You're a mean son-of-a-bitch!" she tells me. And then she hangs up.

I didn't see or hear from her the whole day.

The *next* morning at nine-thirty?

Yep, you guessed it.

"*Pleeease!*"

So I get round there. Megan's pretty shaken-up, all trembly, by this time. And yes, her curtains are shredded up pretty badly. So I try to think this through.

"Cats usually leave a smell," I tell her. "But there isn't one. Can you find any fur?"

We looked, and didn't.

"You could try, like, sprinkling talcum powder on the floor, seeing if it leaves any paw marks?"

But she's too freaked to get her head round anything sensible right now, and she keeps clinging on to me, and this time we do end up making out, at ten-fifteen in the morning. Just call that striking a blow for the ordinary working man.

Some time mid-afternoon, Megan shows up in the store and says, "I want some books on ghosts."

"Say what?"

"It's a ghost-cat. It's the only thing it can be. And I want a book on exorcisms too."

"Don't priests do that?"

"God, Lenny. You know I'm not religious."

So she ends up buying three volumes, using my discount. And when she's gone, Chan Park, the store's joint-owner, comes sauntering across to me with the usual supercilious look on his face.

Now, Chan's a pretty stylish-looking dude, always dressed in leather, with a little moustache and goatee beard that I have to admit look pretty cool on a Korean. And he's very smart, and reads a lot of heavy non-fiction stuff. But he does have airs and graces. Yeah right, like he thinks nobody knows he drops so many E's at the weekend he'd end up humping Genghis Khan if Genghis Khan smiled at him nicely.

"So, Leonard," he says. "It seems your barely legal girlfriend has wigged out completely."

Which is designed to annoy me and does, since he's always making snide remarks about Megan's age. But I don't respond. In the first place, I'm already in the dog-house for the second late-show in a week. And in the second, I have this theory by now, and maybe Chan's the right person to try it out on.

I explain what's been going on, and he keeps looking at me like I'm on something.

"Do you agree with her, about the ghost stuff?"

"No, man. She's a Goth, and Goths believe in that shit. What I think, see, is that there's this kind of alternate world, just like ours but different, and —"

"Leonard?" Chan just snaps. "Would you spare me all the Star Trek bullshit? Yes, okay I'll admit, quantum theory does point to the probability of separate planes of existence. But they're kept apart, quite strongly I'd imagine. I'd suggest it would take the force of something like a black hole to break through. And do you think a fucking cat would go to all that trouble just to shred your little girlfriend's curtains?"

I had to admit that didn't sound too likely.

"But I'll tell you what it might be, though."

And he's gone ever so slightly smirky now, so that I can't tell whether he's jerking my chain or not.

But he starts to tell me all about this dude called Professor Stephen Hawking. I think I saw him on the tv once — he's the guy who talks funny, right? And apparently, this guy has figured out how much the entire galaxy weighs —

"How did he do *that?* I mean, that's *impossible!*"

Chan rolls his eyeballs up before continuing.

And has realised that there isn't enough mass — I

think I've got this right — to create enough gravity to hold the whole fuck-wad together. So he gets this idea that there might be other stuff out there called Dark Matter, which we can't see or touch. And there are other scientists who are looking for it now, and some of them even think they've found some.

I almost burst in with *how?* again, but my head's throbbing a little and I'm waiting for Chan to get to the point.

"Think about this." And he's grinning openly by now. "If there is Dark Matter, why should it just be like dust, floating in space? I'm made of matter. So are you. So's that delivery you haven't unpacked yet."

"I guess so."

"And so, why shouldn't Dark Matter form real, even living objects? Like cats?"

And he walks off grinning like he's just made out with Brad Pitt *and* Brad Pitt's cloned twin brother.

I was pretty sure that he *was* mostly yanking my chain. But knowing Chan and the way he likes to air his knowledge, I was also pretty sure that that Dark Matter stuff was based in fact.

My head was still throbbing slightly by the time we closed up, and I thought about it all the way to Megan's. Matter that wasn't there, but was? Non-existent stuff that some egg-head could prove did exist? Wow, the world just kept on getting weirder, and science wasn't exactly helping matters any.

When Megan opened the door, there were, like, a hundred thousand candles lit up all behind her. And she was clutching a bible which she'd borrowed from the Baptist spinster two floors down.

"I am *never* going to get her off my back now," Megan complained. "She kept asking if I want to go to church."

Anyway, the whole point was — as you've probably guessed — she was about to perform an exorcism, and was waiting for yours truly to join in. I tried explaining to her about Dark Matter, but she didn't buy it, not a bit.

"Weighed the *galaxy?*" she kept on saying. "That's such total bullshit!"

So we did the whole Rod Steiger bit. No one's head span around. No one chucked. Nothing at all happened, except I practically set fire to my pants when I stepped backwards into a row of candles. But at the end of it, Megan had a strange, satisfied look on her face, calm like. "It's gone," she told me. "I can feel things like that."

Like I keep on pointing out, she *is* a Goth.

I decided to do the noble, gentlemanly thing, though.

"Look, I'll stay over tonight, just to make sure everything's gone back to normal."

"Sounds nice."

And she starts rubbing up against me, so I have to push her back a little.

"No! You know what'll happen if we do that. I'll fall flat asleep afterwards. I have to stay, like, focussed."

Typically of Megan, though, she doesn't let it go at that, and it doesn't take long before I succumb. But I force myself to get up straight away when we're done, since I have a duty to perform tonight. Think tough. Think steely. Think Clint Eastwood in that movie where he's protecting the President, 'The Bodyguard'. Shit, no, that's Kevin Costner.

"Coffee, wench," I command Megan.

And she honestly doesn't mind. She's got this special glow about her now.

"Are you really going to stay up all night?"

"I hope so, just to make sure. Have you got some ups?"

Of course she did. It's the way Goth chicks stay so thin.

Anyway, there I am at four in the morning, sitting at the foot of Megan's bed. And Megan's snoring really loudly — Jesus! And my eyelids are starting to get heavy, and I don't really want to take *another* up — I, you know, have my health to think of. So I force myself. Show true grit. Real, rigid determination.

'In The Line of Fire,' *that's* the one.

And guess what, I did it. Stayed awake the whole way through till dawn. You didn't think I had it in me, did you?

So the daylight starts shining through Megan's thin, shredded curtains.

And there are huge parallel scratches on the plaster of the wall beneath them.

Megan goes berserk when she wakes up.

"You fell asleep! For God's sake!"

"No I didn't."

"You must have done!"

But I know what the truth is. And I'm realising something else as well. Not just that I didn't see anything. There wasn't a sound. And you'd have heard a scritching as the claws went down the plaster, at the very least.

So I keep thinking . . . Dark Matter! Stuff that actually exists, but isn't there.

And the next thing, there's this awful noise from out back. Megan and I both rush to the kitchen window, just in time to see a gruesome sight.

The downstairs window of the block behind is open. And through it, we can see the old lady who owns Mr. Paws. Or *thought* she did. Because Mr. Paws is all over her face, scratching and yowling. And she's screaming her head off.

After a few seconds of this, Mr. Paws lets go and and jumps out through the window, where he prowls around the little courtyard, his back arched, all snarly.

And this from a cat who wouldn't move a muscle if you stuck a knife up its fat ass.

"What's got *into* him?" Megan asks, her voice extremely quivery now.

"I don't know."

An ambulance came after a while. And then a couple of guys with long thick gloves, who still had a hell of a time getting Mr. Paws into a basket.

After that, everything just calmed down flat to normal. Megan was still somewhat freaked, but if I was late for work again I knew that Chan would fire me.

I thought about it all day, though. And this is what I half-way figured. Look, it must be cool in some ways being a Dark Matter cat. You can move about and do stuff without anyone being able to stop you. Hell, if I was a Dark Matter Leonard Melnic —

Well, you get the picture.

But it must get pretty boring after a while. Like, wouldn't it be better to have an actual real body and be able to do realer stuff?

Where did the body come from though? Could Dark Matter and ... er ... Mattery Matter exist in the same place?

Mr. Paws?

And the way that he behaved? Well, it seemed to make sense that Dark Matter creatures would have a dark nature.

I didn't go back to Megan's that evening, because the idea freaked me out too much.

But at eight P.M., the phone goes.

"THERE'S SOMEONE in here!"

"The cat?"

"No, a person! I can't see her! But she's in the bathroom, moving stuff around!"

"Fuck Megan, just get *out* of there, right now!"

I only begin wondering why Meg called the intruder 'she' after I've put the phone down. Since ... she couldn't see who it was, and intruders are usually 'he'.

Maybe she sensed something.

As I said at the beginning of this, it is ten minutes to Megan's. More like five if you're moving fast.

Twenty fucking minutes passed before I saw her shadowy figure coming down the street. Twenty God-almighty friggit minutes during which I paced and clenched and almost went insane.

So I throw open my window, and I'm about to ask her where she's been, when I see that there's a big bag thrown over her shoulder.

"You *packed?*"

She looks up at me, but I can't see her features.

"I've got some expensive stuff! I'm not insured, you know!"

"You fucking *packed,* with an intruder in your place?"

"Don't talk to me like that! I'm coming up!"

About half a minute later, I can hear her footsteps

coming up the stairs, and I'm reaching for my door-knob —

A<small>ND</small> I'M STILL THERE now, with my hand half-way towards it, but not moving.

Megan's banging on the door, and saying the same things over and over. They started out whiney-bewildered, and then whiney-frightened. Now she's sounding whiney-cross.

"Lenn-iieee? Please! Let me in! Lenny, what are you *doing?*"

I'm not listening to the words any more. Just to the tone of her voice. Trying to detect something.

What?

Like . . . sly. Deceptive.

Something . . . just not right.

You see, I may not be any Professor Stephen Hawking, but I've figured out one thing for myself.

If there really are such things as non-existent cats, then a lot of them, without a doubt, have non-existent owners. 🐾

Tony Richards tells us that he's never kept pets himself — "I'm just away from home too much. But the cats of neighbours have always played a large part of my life down the years, all those Smokies, Snoopies, and Misties coming nosing around my place to see what I'm up to. Curiosity killed the cat? The ones who live near me seem to thrive on it. It's that quality, plus their energy and occasional capacity of mischief, that was part of the inspiration for this story."

NON-EXISTENT CATS

ANGELIQUE'S

by Sandra Beswetherick

B EN STOOD in the graveled lot of the roadside café, unbelieving. Gone were the window boxes over-flowing with petunias and geraniums, gone the bright, freshly-painted look of the building.

Even the overhead sign was now missing letters; **ANGELIQUE'S** reduced to **ANGEL'S**.

He opened the café's door, and no ginger cat jumped down from its chair to wind about his legs and meow a greeting. The air smelled of cigarettes and fryer grease.

"I'm looking for Angelique." Ben raised his voice to be heard above the football match playing on the widescreen.

"Don't know any Angelique," answered the burly man behind the bar.

"You must know her! This was her café. Ange-lique's." His voice sounded desperate even in his own ears.

The café had been a wreck of a building when she'd bought it. Financed by a loan from a well-to-do aunt who had considered it a wise investment in her niece's future. Angelique had credited her cat Thomas with its discovery. "You knew exactly what I wanted,

Thomas. Always looking out for me, aren't you?" Ben laughed at Angelique's attributing Thomas with an uncanny nature, and she laughed with him. Thomas's leading Angelique to the site — albeit in a merry chase — remained a puzzle, though. According to Angelique, the site was far beyond Thomas's territory, and it was unlikely he'd been there before.

"Are you sure you want to do this," Ben had asked, surveying the broken windows, the sagging ceiling, and warped floor. "Oh yes," Angelique had answered, a fierce, determined gleam in her eye. "This is only the beginning, the first big step." And he'd helped her rip out the inside of that place and rebuild it to her specifications .With Thomas supervising from his perch on a ladder, meowing his encouragement, ensuring they always broke for lunch.

Once, when Ben and Thomas were alone, Angelique running an errand, Ben had turned round and found Thomas sitting on his perch staring at him with narrowed, unblinking eyes. The hairs on the back of Ben's neck had pricked. Was the cat more than he seemed? Then Thomas had flicked a paw at a passing moth and became nothing more than a cat again.

"Look, what do you want from me?" the bartender demanded of Ben. "I'm the hired help, okay? I started six months ago." He went back to washing glasses. "The place was Angel's then."

Ben turned, pushed open the door, and stepped back into the graveled parking lot. He'd been gone too long, he thought, he'd returned too late. His reasons for leaving seemed trivial now.

"I need to get away from here," he'd told Angelique. Had it been three years ago? Her future was assured by then, her café more popular than even he could have imagined. "This town's too small, and there's so much out there I want to see." He'd held her close, this home-town girl who was so special. "I can't promise I'll be back," he'd said, not wanting her to feel she had to wait for him. "I understand," she'd whispered in her ear. As he'd left she'd stood in the doorway of her little café, her beloved cat Thomas cradled in her arms, her eyes shimmering with unshed tears.

His first few months on the road had been exhilarating.

Long stretches of empty highway that disappeared into spectacular sunsets. Azure, snow-capped ranges hovering on a distant horizon. White surf surging against a rocky shoreline. Big cities with bright lights and their fast-paced lifestyle. New places, new faces, new experiences. They'd help blot out thoughts of Angelique.

The months kept sliding by while he moved about the map, taking one job after the other. His latest occupation was driving transports long distance. As the number of miles accumulated, though, and more time slipped by, he found himself, inexplicably, growing increasingly restless. The urge to move on hit him hardest in the evenings. The feeling that down the road or in the next town, he'd find something bigger, better, more satisfying.

WHEN HE spotted a ginger cat looking up at his hotel window one night, "Thomas!" burst out of him so unexpectedly, it surprised even himself. But the jammed window refused to budge, and by the time he'd raced downstairs, there was no sign of the cat. "Thomas?"

He laughed at himself, then. Thomas was hundreds of miles behind him. The cat had simply been another ginger cat. Ben shook his head over his inexplicable reaction and returned to his room, blaming the ache in his chest on the pizza he'd bolted for lunch.

He was eating supper in a roadside tavern the next time he saw a ginger cat. He looked up and choked on his mouthful of chicken. The cat was sitting on the hood of his transport serenely washing its face with a paw. Ben raced for the door, pushing past the proprietor who snatched at his sleeve. "Hey, you haven't paid." When he reached the transport, the cat had vanished. Ben searched for paw prints which should have marked the hood and the thick dust on the ground. There were none, and he determinedly dismissed the cat as a figment of his imagination brought on by fatigue.

Over the next few weeks Ben saw or thought he saw a ginger cat almost every time he turned around. Especially late evenings. A blur of orange caught by the corner of his eye. An orange tail disappearing round a corner.

The night he saw a ginger cat sitting on the front steps of a house, he'd had enough. He slammed the brakes so hard his transport almost slithered into the ditch. The cat continued to stare at him, the tip of its tail twitching. "Thomas!" Ben shouted. It had the same white chest, the same white front paw. Ben tried to keep it in sight as he clambered out the driver's side and raced round the front of his truck. But when he reached the front walk of the house, the step was empty.

Ben hammered on the door. He had to know what was going on. Were there that many ginger cats in the world? "I want to ask about your cat," he said to the woman who opened the door. "We don't have a cat," she answered.

"A neighbor's cat, then, or a stray. Big, ginger cat with a white chest and one white front paw." He was out of breath, his heart racing.

"I haven't seen a cat like that around. Why? Have you lost one?"

The question brought Ben up short. As if someone had held up a stop sign and the brakes of his truck had locked. Had he lost a cat? Had he lost a cat and something more? He couldn't deny any longer that the ache in his chest each time the cat appeared was really a stab of loneliness. That the reason he always saw the cat as Thomas was that Angelique would have been close by.

Ben climbed back into the cab of his truck. He would make this final delivery and then turn round. What he'd been restlessly searching for didn't lie ahead of him but behind. He couldn't wait to get back to Angelique's.

Now, here he was outside the café, and he'd arrived too late. Even the shutters hung crooked on the café's dirty windows. Had he lost Angelique forever? Had she married and moved away? He suppressed the thought that something terrible had had happened to her.

The evening's chill and damp seeped into him, and Ben hugged himself for warmth. He'd never felt so alone, so bereft. He'd held the café's image in his mind as never changing, with Angelique forever standing in the doorway cradling Thomas.

When a ginger cat disappeared into the alley up the street, Ben almost missed it. Was it his imagination again? Another subconscious desire? Or this time was it really — "Thomas? Thomas, wait!" He raced up the street.

The alley was deserted. "Thomas!" he called all the same, the stabbing ache unbearable.

Round the corner of a building at the alley's far end, the ginger cat appeared. It studied him with pale eyes. "Thomas?" Ben whispered. The cat meowed. Then it trotted toward him, tail high in recognition. Ben gathered the cat up and felt the deep rumble of its contentment. "Thomas, old man, you don't now how good it is to see you." The cat butted Ben's chin with its head, as pleased, it seemed, to see Ben.

"Where's Angelique? How'd she lose the café? I'll do anything to get it back for her."

"Anything?" a familiar voice laughed. Ben turned round. "Will you mop floors and wait tables?" Angelique asked.

Ben set Thomas down. Then Angelique was in his arms, and nothing had ever felt so right, so good.

"Anything," he whispered, not wanting to let her go, breathing in the familiar, sweet scent of her hair, feeling the warmth of her body. "Anything and everything as long as we are together." She kissed him then and melted away the cold ache in his heart. "I've missed you," he said.

Then Angelique took his hand. "Are you hungry? I'll cook supper, and then you can tell me where you've been, all that you've done, and all you've seen."

Ben let himself be led, Thomas going before them. "I knew you'd come back to me. But Thomas was growing anxious. You'd been gone so long. He's been out almost every night of late, looking for you, I think, worried you were lost and wouldn't find us."

Thomas now sat on the back veranda of a large Victorian house, looking both regal and smug. "He has?" Ben shot the cat a bewildered look. Thomas's smile was inscrutable.

"I . . . when I saw what had become of the café . . ." Ben tore his gaze away from the cat. "I didn't know what to think. I thought the café was your life."

"Don't you remember me saying the café was only the beginning?"

She opened the back door, and Ben found himself in a kitchen, with copper pots hanging overhead, tantalizing aromas rising from steaming pots, a cook filling plates that were carried away by waiters. He caught a glimpse through an open door of couples seated round linen- draped tables, dining in the soft glow of candlelight. "I sold the café in order to buy this place. It now belongs to me and the bank."

Ben burst out laughing. Here he'd assumed something dreadful. That he'd been seeing the ginger cat as a cry for help, that Angelique needed rescue.

"I wouldn't have known to look for you here," he admitted, embarrassed he'd underestimated Angelique so badly.

"Of course you would have," she insisted. "Angelique's had to stay with the café, but I named the restaurant with your finding us in mind." She pointed at the bib of her white apron. Below the embroidered figure of an orange cat, printed in gold letters, was a name Ben knew would have surely drawn him. **CHEZ THOMAS.**   🐾

Sandra Beswetherick's short stories have appeared in magazines published in Australia, Great Britain, the USA, and Sweden. Her story "The Twilight Zone on the Rideau Canal" is part of the Canadian mystery anthology Locked Up, *launches in April 2007. San-*

ANGELIQUE'S

dra lives near Seeley's Bay, Ontario, with her hus-
band and two cats. They share their property with
deer, coyote, the odd skunk, and several raccoons.

3 HAIKU

by Mark Budman

You have more names
Than a Spanish grandee. Your lives
I'm too envious to count.

Your eyes change colors
Like a girl's moods. Circe!
Turn me into a mouse.

Your paws weave time
Oh, awaiting Penelope!
Your Tom will return

THE CAT

by Charles Baudelaire

Come, my beautiful cat, to my amorous core;
Retract your claws inside your paws
And let me plunge into your wise eyes once more
That are mingled of agate and metals.

When my fingers caress at leisure
Your head and your back's elasticity
And when my hand's become drunk with pleasure
From your palpating electricity.

I see my woman in spirit. Her regard,
Like yours, amiable beast,
Profound and cold, cuts and cracks like a sword;

And, from her head to her feet,
A delicate look, a dangerous perfume
Swims around her brown body's bloom.

BLACK PUMPS & A SKANKY TOM

by Pat Esden

FERP DIDN'T MIND living in the camper trailer that the selectmen had set up for him behind the fairgrounds. He didn't mind it, but he liked sitting on Church Street watching traffic better than staring out a window at the vacant grandstand.

No one had actually told him he couldn't spend his days hanging around downtown. They just said that with winter coming he'd freeze to death living on the streets.

Ferp turned on the faucet and studied his hands as he washed them, rough as a boar's ass, but even after ten years on the streets he didn't have any frozen fingers. You didn't survive by being stupid; his Pappy had taught him that. And he weren't stupid enough to believe the winter cold had spurred the selectman's generosity. The coming of the leaf-peeping tourists and the ski crowd had made them want to get him off the streets.

But he weren't about to complain, that wasn't the generous thing for him to do. Let the selectmen feel compassionate; after all he didn't really mind the camper. It didn't suffocate him like living in a house did.

And there were the cats.

Ferp reached up over the sink, took down the box of powered milk and shook a couple of cupfuls into a galvanized pan. The state gave the stuff out for free on the 15th of every month. He held the pan under the faucet, slowly adding water to the powered milk — awful stuff, but the cats liked it.

Scuffing across the braided rug, Ferp opened the camper door. The frosty air clung in his nostrils as he shouted. "Punky, punky, punky!" No need to call them twice. The critters appeared from everywhere: blacks, calicos, tabbies, and a couple of cats so ragged-up from fighting it was hard to tell what they had started out looking like.

Ferp yanked on his left pants leg to help his bum knee raise and lower as he stepped down onto the pallet that served as his stoop. He set down the pan of milk and bent over to examine the gifts the cats had left for him in the night: a mouse head, a thin bit of intestine, a chickadee's wing, and a charge card —

Now that made no sense.

He picked up the thin rectangle of plastic, turning it over and holding it out so he could read it without his glasses. No, not a charge card: it had a picture of a bus on the front with a bar code on the back, mangled up a bit, but definitely a bus pass.

Probably the pass was no good, but instead of tossing it into the garbage can, he slid it in his pocket. With the cats rubbing and slurping at his feet, it didn't feel right to just toss the gift away — one of them had gone through the trouble of bringing it to him . . . and now that he paid attention to the cats, he could see which one.

A gray tom with patchy fur and one ear crusted in scabs, sat straight as a poker, watching him as if waiting for a thank you. No, not a thank you. The skanky tom wanted to tell him something.

The tomcat stared at the pocket where Ferp had stashed the pass, then glanced over his shoulder.

"What are you saying?" Ferp asked the tom.

The tom turned and trotted a few feet toward the distant grandstand, shaking his tail like a rattlesnake.

"If you want someone to go for a walk with you, wait until after breakfast," Ferp said and then he remembered that the last time he'd explored around the grandstand on a Sunday morning he'd found a pint of Old Duke. Some kids probably had misplaced the bottle the night before. Not that he blamed them for forgetting the wine. If he had a hot little girl under the grandstand, he might even forget his booze. Well, that was if it was ten or fifteen years ago, back when he was a kid too.

Ferp followed the tomcat across the rutted racetrack, to the grandstand.

Fresh tire tracks, dual like those of a big truck, stopped on the west side. Where the truck had turned around a pair of turquoise underpants decorated the soft earth.

He didn't remember hearing any trucks or cars last night, but he'd been sleeping with Duke of grapes and nothing usually woke him then.

Claws raked Ferp's pants. He swung his foot, but the tom dashed off before he could hoist its butt. The damn thing only trotted out of range, then looked back and yowled.

"Okay cat, it's your game."

The tom circled something. In the grass by the grandstand a shoe lay, a black pump, the kind Mama used to wear. The tom rubbed his chin on the shoe.

Ferp shook his head. "You find the other one, we might get fifty cent for them down at the clothes exchange, but a single shoe's a bust. No sense wasting time here."

Leaving the tom behind, Ferp hobbled back to the camper, chugged down a mug of the good stuff, then headed for Church Street and St. Mary's.

This time of year, the sun hit St. Mary's steps at 10:00 A.M. With mass getting out at 10:30 that allowed him time to relax and catch his breath before he started hustling the Catholic crowd for change.

by Pat Esden

Ferp grunted down onto the bottom step and stretched out his legs. He leaned forward, squinting. On the far side of the sidewalk, a bulging newspaper rack sat next to a light pole. He could just make out the headlines through the wire-reinforced glass:

MISSING GIRL'S BODY FOUND
LOCAL MAN ARRESTED

The pictures below the headline caught his attention.

He lurched to his feet and stared at the newspaper. The pictures showed a woman's dark colored pump, a bus pass, and a cell phone. The caption read: **Police Seek Evidence.** He touched his pants pocket, making sure he hadn't lost the thin rectangle of plastic. Could it be the pass they were looking for?

His pappy's voice rattled through Ferp's head. *Keep your mouth shut.*

Ferp closed his eyes, shutting out the voice. The cops had found the dead girl, they had a suspect in jail — they just needed to find the evidence. He wasn't telling on no one.

A twinge of pain jabbed his knee. *Them that says things get hurt.*

Ferp massaged the hurt from his knee and dared another glance at the paper. On the bottom of the page was a formal photo of a high school girl. He'd show the cops the bus pass, but just that for now. . . .

Behind him, the doors of St. Mary's creaked open and organ music rose. If he left now, he'd miss the Catholics. And at a minimum they were good for ten bucks: three bottles of Old Duke. He shifted his weight onto his good leg and scratched his chin. Then huffed out his breath and started up Church Street, a bit more lickety-split than he usually liked.

By the time Ferp reached the police station he could hardly breathe. The way he wheezed, you would have thought he had asthma like Mama had.

Pappy had always said, *if Mama didn't shriek so much, she wouldn't have that damn breathing problem.*

BLACK PUMPS & A SKANKY TOM

Ferp shook his head. He weren't like Mama; he weren't going to die of not breathing.

He sucked in a long breath and yanked on the police station door.

It didn't open.

He squinted at the blackened window glass and jabbed the buzzer.

A grainy voice he recognized spat back at him. "Is that you, Ferp?" Jolene said.

He could picture her behind the tall counter, her black eyes far too small to be human, skinny legs, her high heels tap, tap tapping across the police station floor.

Mama's shoes clicked like that. But not when she came home late at night; then she carried her shoes; and her feet went pad, pad, pad across the linoleum.

Jolene's voice came again. "I got better things to do than play games with you."

"I found something," Ferp said.

"That's nice," Jolene replied.

Something brushed Ferp's leg: the damn tomcat. It must have followed him. He reached down to touch the tip of the tom's tail. The cat ducked out of reach.

Ferp rang the buzzer again. "I found some of that murdered girl's stuff." He waved the bus pass and re-alized he had said more than he had intended to. He rubbed the back of his neck. Had she noticed what he said?

The tomcat clawed at his pants. Behind him the traffic whirred. What was taking her so long?

Damn Jolene. He rang again. "I got the bus pass with me."

"Wait a minute," Jolene answered.

He set the pass on the concrete window ledge and squished his face against the glass. He could see her skinny ass shimmying out from behind the counter and disappearing down the hall.

From behind him came the screech of tires.

Ferp swung round.

A minivan and a BMW swerved into the far lane to avoid hitting the tomcat.

The tom stopped on the center line. He licked a paw, then glanced at Ferp.

It weren't really *his* cat, but right now it felt that way. And big trouble was coming from both directions: to the right a line of cars clamored into the street from St. Mary's parking lot and to the left a milk truck and a tractor trailer loomed.

Ferp dashed into the street.

Horns blared.

The milk truck slowed.

"Damn drunk," someone shouted.

"Get out of the road."

A car squealed past.

Ferp scooped the cat off the centerline. The sloppy weight of the tom surprised him. Then again, *trouble never is light,* his pappy said that too, said it lots before he died two years ago.

Ferp tottered across the far lane and down the gutter until he found a break in the curb. With his hands full of tomcat he couldn't grab his pants leg in order to bend his knee and get up the high curb.

He balanced the tom on one hip, holding him tight, while he felt his pocket.

Empty. He'd left the bus pass on the window sill.

Ferp glanced up the street at the police station. No one had come out yet.

Scratching behind the tom's scabby ear, he mulled over the situation. He hadn't considered it before; but if old Chief Scranton was on duty today, he might not come out at all. Scranton didn't have much use for him.

Ferp smacked his dry lips. It would have been nice to have a nip of the Duke right now. He clutched the wiggling tomcat tighter and kept an eye on the station.

Watching, came natural to him. Pappy always said it were better to watch.

Watch yourself boy, keep your mouth shut. Them that says things get hurt. You know what hurting is don't ya?

With his free hand, Ferp touched his knee. *Yup Pappy, I know.* And at the same moment, as if to reinforce the point, the tomcat dug in his claws. *Spawn of the devil, just like Pappy.*

Ferp dropped the tom.

The tom glared up at him, his good ear swiveling. He looked back at the street, then sauntered to the curb and yowled.

Out of the corner of his eye, Ferp saw the door of the police station open and Chief Scranton step out, his hat in his hand, his grayed hair spiked like a porcupine.

Scranton picked up the bus pass from the window ledge.

The tom crouched as if about to jump back into the street. Ferp lunged and grabbed the cat by its scruff. He swung the tom up, so they stared eye to eye. "Is there a reason you want to kill yourself, or are you just trying to keep me from going to the cops?"

Watch yourself boy, keep your mouth shut. Them that says things get hurt. You know what hurting is don't ya?

Ferp studied the cat's eyes. "If you didn't want me to take the pass to the cops, why did give it to me?" He was talking to a damn cat; now that was crazy.

Crazy like talking to Scranton.

A shiver prickled up Ferp's spine as he recalled a Sunday ten years ago, back when Chief Scranton was called Sergeant Scranton and he had come to the house to talk to Pappy.

Ferp had stood stock-still against the refrigerator.

With his hands clasped behind his back, Scranton had glared at Pappy.

Ferp wondered how come lying came so natural to Pappy. Pappy's voice shook. "You can't find her anywhere?" His shoulders trembled. "You've dredged the lake?"

Scranton raised an eyebrow. "You sure your wife didn't run off with someone?"

Pappy scratched at his scabby ear. "We had a time early on when she wandered." He shook his head. "I went to the doctor and got me some pills. Fixed me up so I can go all night — that cured her of cheating."

"Yeh, right," the corner of Scranton's mouth twisted

with cynicism. "Speaking of doctors, you might want to get a doctor to look at that boy of yours." He brought his arms out from behind his back and folded them across his chest. "You said it was a baseball hit him upside the knee?"

Ferp looked away as Scranton's eyes met his. He never was as good as Pappy at the lying. And if Scranton stared at him long enough he'd see things he shouldn't. See Pappy swinging the pipe. Maybe even hear the crunching sound of the pipe hitting his knee. *Them that says things get hurt. This ain't nothing compared to real hurting?* That's what Pappy had said right after he swung the pipe.

Drawing in a deep breath, Ferp brought himself back to the here and now. He glanced once more at the police station. Jolene came out of the door. She and Scranton started talking as they stared off in the wrong direction.

In the wrong direction.

Anger rose from deep inside of Ferp. Even without looking in his eyes you'd have thought Scranton might have asked more questions about his broken knee back then. But not Scranton, he only asked about Mama.

Ferp clutched the tomcat close. He lumbered down the street and into an alleyway. If the bus pass was the one the cops were looking for, if they wanted to question him, then Scranton knew where to find him. And lots of women wore black pumps, and the cat hadn't dragged home a cell phone. Better to stay out of it.

When Ferp got back to the camper, he left the tom on the stoop and went inside. He braced a broom against the door to hold it shut, chugged down a mug of the Duke, and decided to take a nap.

F̲ERP'S EYES snapped open.

Rain tap, tap, tapped on the roof and the dimming light told him late afternoon had come.

A car horn blared.

That must have been what woke him. He tucked his shirt into his pants and hobbled to the door.

Outside, Chief Scranton leaned against the hood of his cruiser, picking at his fingers casually like he hadn't even noticed the cold drizzle.

In the cruiser another man sat on the passenger side and behind him a dog paced, back and forth, barking his head off.

Ferp clomped down onto the stoop.

Scranton frowned. "Jolene tells me, you're the one left the bus pass at the station this morning."

Ferp nodded. His stomach churned. Why had he thought going to the cops was a good idea? If only the cat hadn't given him the pass and shown him the other stuff.

Scranton stood up, brushing off the back of his trousers. "Where'd you find it?"

"On the stoop." Ferp said.

Scranton's eyes narrowed.

Ferp glanced around. The skanky tom sat in the grass beside the cruiser. "That cat brought it to me."

"Yeah, right." Scranton started toward the driver's door of the cruiser. "Don't know why I bothered to drive out here. I knew it was a waste of time."

The cat's tail stood up straight, shaking like a rattler. And for a split second, Ferp thought the cat had a human face. A chill trembled through him. He couldn't have seen that. He must have had a bit too much Duke before his nap.

Chief Scranton opened the cruiser door. "I thought you might have out-grown lying," he mumbled.

Ferp swallowed hard. Scranton's leaving was for the best. He shouldn't have started this, but he wanted to say he it wasn't lying. He should tell Scranton about the shoe and the underpants —

Keep your mouth shut, the words filled his head.

Yup, that's what he would do, Ferp told himself. But before he could hold back, he said, "Was it the girl's pass?"

"Can't be sure. It's too scratched up to read the barcode."

"But it could be?"

"Yeah." Scranton folded his arms across his chest. "Your cat didn't happen to drag in anything else?"

Ferp couldn't figure out if Scranton was being sarcastic or not, so he thought it best not to mention the cat again. "No, but I found some things over by the grandstand, a shoe, underpants, and tire tracks."

Scranton's expression didn't change, but the other man got out of the cruiser. "I think we ought to take a look," the other man said, buttoning up his trench coat.

WHEN THEY GOT to where the tire tracks had been, Ferp found only a slick of mud puddles.

Chief Scranton walked around the puddles. "These are your tire tracks?"

"Dual tires." Ferp said. "And the shoe was right there on the grass."

"But they aren't now." Scranton's brows drew together.

Ferp picked up a stick and stirred a puddle. "The underpants were here." The stick came out empty.

This was useless. What had happened to everything? Had the killer come back? He couldn't have; the paper said the cops had locked the suspect up on other charges.

The man in the trench coat lit a cigarette. "About as much good as the other leads." He turned toward Ferp. "Did you see a cell phone or hear the truck?"

"No." Ferp said. "They were turquoise underpants."

The two cops glanced at each other as if that indeed meant something, then turned away and started talking low.

Ferp went over to where the shoe had been. He squatted down. Nothing, not even bent grass.

The tomcat pushed against his arm and purred.

If the tom hadn't shown him this stuff, he'd never have known it was here. He'd never gone to the police station and wouldn't feel so useless.

Ferp pushed the cat away. "You're the one who started this."

The cat trotted back and rubbed the corner of his mouth on Ferp's leg as if marking him.

"What, you like putting me in a tough spot with the cops, then watching them not believe me?"

Ferp rested his hand on the ground to steady himself. He closed his eyes and tried to remember exactly what the shoe had looked like. But instead of picturing the murdered girl's pumps he saw Mama's shoes.

MAMA'S BLACK PUMPS had lain on the kitchen floor. Beside them, Mama had sprawled on her back, Pappy's knee pressing on her chest, pinning her to the floor.

"This isn't funny, let me up!" she had screeched.

Pappy shifted all his weight onto her chest.

Her arms flailed. She tried to scratch Pappy's face. He turned his head.

Ferp stood against the wall. He couldn't move. He couldn't look away. *Pappy, stop.*

"Help me," Mama cried. She thrashed. Her nails clawed Pappy's ear. And blood trickled down his sideburns.

Ferp's stomach clenched.

Pappy's jaundiced eyes looked up at him. "You have to watch where you leave bruises, son. If I grabbed her wrists the cops would notice it for sure," he said. "They look for that stuff: wives with black eyes, kids with welts and cigarette burns. But we're smarter than them."

Her ragged breath became a wheeze.

Ferp wanted to go to her. He wanted to get her the inhaler. He could see it under the table, stuffed inside one of her black pumps.

Mama's face turned blue. Her wheeze staggered into gasps.

Please Pappy let her up; let her have her medicine.

Pappy leaned close to Mama's face. "It hurts, it hurts bad, doesn't it," he said. "Like knowing your woman's a fucking whore."

Mama's fingers fell open.

Pappy's eyes grew as wild as a feral cat's. "Watch yourself boy, keep your mouth shut. Them that says things get hurt. You know what hurting is don't you?"

Ferp nodded. No, he would never forget what Pappy had said that night.

He SWAGGERED UP from the grass. He had to stop thinking about the past, had to stop doing this to himself. He kicked the spot where the shoe had been, then glanced over to see if the cops had noticed.

Their backs were still to him.

He shouldn't have gotten involved. Him and the Duke were doing just fine without this dead girl, without these cops to get his memories riled up.

In front of him, the cat sat where the shoe had lain, staring up.

Ferp's chest tightened. Now he could see it, the cat didn't have a real human face, just a resemblance: the jaundiced eyes, the patchy grayed hair, the scabby ear. For all the world the tomcat looked like Pappy.

He squinted at the cat. He had never done much thinking about death, the afterlife — about reincarnation. Some people believed in it and if it were true . . . "That's you Pappy, isn't it? You've come back." He could hardly believe it, but it made sense.

The tomcat scratched his scabby ear and stared at the grandstand.

"You know what happened to the girl. You watched him kill her and you're making me a part of it. It's a big joke to you. Watching the hurt. Watching me look like a fool instead of helping." He took a step closer. "When I took my nap, you dragged the stuff off, didn't you?"

The tom shook his tail, then trotted toward Scranton, his paws pad, pad, padding on the damp earth like a woman crossing the kitchen late at night with her shoes in her hand.

Ferp's knee twitched.

As the man in the trench coat started back toward the cruiser, Scranton and the cat marched over to Ferp.

"He's from the FBI." Scranton nodded at the other man. "When Jolene mentioned the bus pass he got all excited." Scranton lowered his voice. "See, he doesn't know you like I do. And I can't very well tell him about your mother; that's a can of worms best left alone."

Scranton's eyes bored into Ferp. "I don't know how your father did it. I don't know where her body is, but I know your dad killed your mother. And you didn't have the balls to stop him. You wouldn't even help me put the bastard in jail."

For a long moment, Ferp couldn't even think. Then he felt the tomcat, staring at him.

Ferp put his hands in his pants pockets and lowered his gaze.

Scranton spat. "Do me one favor, the next time you get the idea in your pickled brain that you can make up for not helping your mother by pretending to help with some other woman's murder, don't bother." He turned his back and strode toward the cruiser.

Ferp opened his mouth, but he couldn't speak.

The tom cat hissed.

Sweat beaded Ferp's temples. Damn. Not this time.

Watch yourself boy, keep your mouth shut. Them that says things get hurt. You know what hurting is don't you?

A bolt of pain lanced Ferp's knee and traveled into his groin. He groaned.

Scranton stopped in his tracks. "You said something?"

And in an instant, it came to Ferp. This pain in his knee wasn't the hurt Pappy had meant. His knee weren't the worst of it. The worst of the hurt was not helping and not telling when you wanted to.

Pushing the pain in his knee aside, Ferp called out to Scranton, saying the words he had longed to say fifteen years ago. "Yeah, I said something. I said that a cop should have known no baseball could hurt a kid's knee like that. I said the cop should have asked the kid when his Pappy wasn't around."

As Scranton turned around, Ferp braced himself for Scranton's anger.

But Scranton's eyes were shut as if he had been praying. "How'd he do it?" Scranton asked.

"I wasn't lying about the shoe or the turquoise underpants. I don't know what hauled them off. And I'm not stupid enough to say it were a cat." Ferp moistened his dry lips with his tongue. "You've just got to look. They couldn't have gone far."

"Where's your mother's body?" Scranton's eyes opened wide.

"I don't know. I seen Pappy do it, but I don't know. Please, I saw the shoe." Ferp's legs trembled. "Pappy held her down. He didn't have to do nothing else. It were the asthma, she couldn't breathe."

Silence hung between them. In the distance the cruiser door creaked open, for an instant the dog's barking grew louder, then it smothered as the door slammed shut.

Finally Scranton spoke, "You're right, I shouldn't have let go so easily, not about your mother, she still haunts me. I shouldn't have given up on you. I just got angry, frustrated with you, and forgot to care —"

"Then do something now," Ferp said. "I saw what I said I did. You need to find the stuff, put this girl's murderer away."

"You sure you saw the shoe?"

"Yes."

Scranton turned toward the cruiser and shouted, "Hey! Let that dog out. He might as well sniff around for a few minutes."

Ferp's heart raced with excitement. "I know every inch of this place. I can show you —"

Scranton clasped his hand behind his back. "I think you should go back to the camper. Let us do our job."

Two HOURS LATER as Ferp stood in the camper's open doorway watching a parade of police cruisers pass by, Scranton sauntered over.

He told Ferp they'd found the shoe shoved into a rat hole and covered with dirt. "I shouldn't tell you this but the dog alerted on stuff all over the place: underpants, a cell phone. It looked like something dragged them off and chewed on them." His eyes bored into Ferp's. "It could have been a cat, like the one that left the bus pass on your doorstep." Scranton lifted an eyebrow. He glanced over his shoulder at the darkening grandstand. "Well, I got to get back to work," he said.

Ferp watched Scranton walk away, then turned to go inside, pulling the door shut behind him. But before the door slammed closed, the skanky tom scooted inside.

Ferp squinted at the cat. "You aren't staying in here; get that idea out of your mind."

The cat stretched out on the braided rug, looking up at the ceiling like he wasn't listening.

Ferp rubbed his chin. The cat wasn't that big. It wouldn't take much. He poured a bowl of wine.

He didn't know nothing about reincarnation, but if — despite having a new body — Pappy still was into causing pain and hurt in people's lives, then he probably still had a hankering for wine like he did as a human.

Ferp carried the bowl over to the tomcat. "I'm sorry Pappy, I had to convince the cops to keep looking for that stuff; that girl weren't like Mama; she weren't no whore." His throat tightened as he said it, but he kept his voice steady.

After setting the bowl on the floor, Ferp slumped down beside the tomcat, stroking the cat as it lapped up the wine.

You don't survive by being stupid. That's what you always said, Pappy, Ferp thought as the cat finished the wine and curled up.

Ten minutes later, the cat began to snore, a high wheezing noise like Mama had made when her asthma came on. The rattling noise filled Ferp's head with thoughts. . . . And he found himself staring at the broom. It weren't much different in size than the pipe Pappy had used on his knee. The wheezing. The broom. The pipe. The skanky tom passed out on the rug.

Ferp swaggered to his feet. He trundled across the braided rug to where the broom stood by the door. Wrapping his fingers around the broom's handle, he picked it up and held it like a baseball bat. He eyed Pappy —

And then lowered the bat, he needed to consider this reincarnation thing. Maybe knowing Pappy was inside a cat was a whole lot better than guessing where and in what shape Pappy might show up in his next life. Who knew if cats really had nine lives?

But, then again, it sure would feel good. He hefted the bat and stepped closer to the tomcat —

Behind Ferp a knock reverberated.

He lowered the broom and leaned it against the wall.

Opening the door, Ferp found Scranton waiting on the stoop, a white bakery bag in one hand and a cup of coffee in the other. He held them out to Ferp. "Sorry to bother you again, but the bakery sent up a load of food for us. Thought you might like some."

Ferp took the offering. "Thanks."

Scranton turned to leave, then stopped, and glanced back at Ferp. "I know I can't make up for what happened to you. But if you ever need anything . . ." His voice trailed off as if he were sincere, but expected his offer not to be taken seriously.

Ferp forced a smile. Then a thought came to him. "There is something you can do."

Scranton's eyes widened.

"I know it sounded stupid when I said a cat dragged that bus pass up here and I know you mentioned it a bit ago to make me feel better." Ferp pointed at the sleeping tom. "But that's the cat I thought left it. And when you said a cat might have dragged the evidence around it got me thinking how that's the sort of thing Pappy might do to make me look stupid and watch me hurting and feel useless like he use to. I know that kind of thinking is crazy. But if it weren't, if things did get reincarnated, then that tom over there might really be Pappy come back to life." He paused to gauge Scranton's reaction.

Scranton's expression remained sincere. "And if it were possible?" he asked.

"Then I was thinking you could use a tomcat down at the police station. An inside cat, one Jolene could pretty up with a collar, have declawed, maybe cut his nuts. But most of all, I'd feel better if I knew that cat was staying locked inside. I'm not saying I believe in reincarnation, just —"

Scranton's eyes stared beyond Ferp toward the tom.

"I'm not sure it isn't possible. You want me to take him right now?"

Ferp stepped inside the camper. He set the coffee and the bakery bag by the sink. "Better now than later, he's not feeling too much pain at the moment." He picked Pappy up, scratched him once behind his scabby ear and handed him to Scranton. "Make sure he doesn't get out, you know Church Street's a busy place, especially with the tourists and the ski crowd."

Pat Esden can be found at her country store in northern Vermont designing with flowers and selling anything that holds still long enough to bring in a coin. When no one's buying, she is either cavorting with her husband and dogs or is in the attic working on her current project, a series of fantasy novels set in present-day New England and upstate New York — with a few side trips to Unseelie Court and the realm of the Crane-king.

Pat's stories can also be read in Challenging Destiny #23 *and* Mythic Circle # 27.

by Pat Esden

DRAGON DREAMS

by Shereen Vedam

MRS. McTAVISH'S daughter drove up as Marina shut the trunk of her Fiat. Marina gave the daughter a quick rundown on what had happened with her mother's dog.

"Finally, good!" she said in a quiet voice, looking over her shoulder where her mother's house appeared dilapidated in the glare of moonlight. Broken furniture was piled haphazardly on the porch. Paint was peeling off the siding and the roof buckled in disrepair.

"My mom couldn't afford him," the daughter continued. "Several times I've given her money for groceries only to come by a few days later and find the cupboard stocked with dog food and nothing for her. She's got no common sense when it comes to animals."

Marina, who had her own strong opinion on this subject, kept her peace and bid the daughter goodnight. She got into her car and waited for Puddy, a black and white feline, to jump in. He scrambled over her lap and settled down on the passenger seat. She petted him and then leaned past him to scratch the all-black cat, Salisha, lying in front of the passenger seat. On the darkened floor, the petting was done more by touch than sight. Marina took a moment to cherish the warm, furry, and *alive* feel of them both before straightening up to back out of the driveway.

A look over her shoulder before leaving showed Mrs. McTavish and her daughter at the front door watching Marina drive away. The daughter had her arm solicitously around her mother, but Marina suspected the sympathy might not be enough to see the old woman through this night of loss and sorrow.

On the highway, Marina floored it. The little car whizzed up the newly paved surface to the symphony of protest wails from Salisha and contented purrs from Puddy.

"I hate this life," she told the cats. "That dog should not have become sick that quickly. Lack of proper care is what killed him, not the disease. Mrs. McTavish can barely support herself. What made her think she had the right to take ownership of an animal that would depend on her for care and feeding for the rest of its life?" She leaned her head out the window and gave vent to her frustration by shouting, "People like her shouldn't be allowed to own a pet!"

MARINA yelped as she tripped over a rock. The bright orange light from the two suns blinded her as she tried to re-orient herself from moving swiftly in her Fiat along a Florida highway one moment, and then standing in a clearing at the edge of a forest the next. Her two cats were still with her, sitting up calmly, but swaying a little as if they too had experienced a shift. But what had happened to her car?

"You guys okay?" she asked, bending to pet each cat with reassuring strokes.

A shadow passed overhead followed by a roar. Startled, she glanced up to see a dragon swoop overhead past them and scorch nearby treetops with a fiery breath.

The cats, smart beasts, reacted first. They raced for the underbrush. She sprinted after them. The dragon swung away with a strong flap of its leathery wings. The resulting wind almost knocked Marina off her feet. On its second pass, it looked as if it was heading straight for them. Fortunately, they'd crossed the border into the woods.

She dodged around branches and brush that the cats leaped over. An overgrown root tripped her. She fell, calling out in alarm as she rolled along the sloping forest floor, dried pine needles stinging her arms and face. A huge blue spruce brought her to a jarring halt. Her last coherent thought was, why had there been two suns in the sky?

At THE SOUND of an annoying, repetitious beep, Marina opened her eyes. Peach walls, starched white sheets, and that clean disinfectant smell suggested she was in a hospital. The high bed with bars on either side of her that she was lying on certainly defied any other explanation. Still, she couldn't help searching for signs of a flying dragon, two suns, or at the very least, those prickly pine needles. The room was spotless and bare except for the bed and a small steel side table with a bed pan on top.

Sighing with relief, she tried to sit up, then groaned as bruises made themselves felt all over her body. Gingerly, she lay back down.

The door opened and a nurse entered. "And how are we this morning, Dr. Preston?" the nurse asked in a cheerful tone.

"*We* have a headache."

"Now, now. Mustn't be testy," the nurse replied. "*We* have some medication right here for you." Her eyes twinkled as she continued, "*We* were just waiting until *we* woke up before bringing it in."

Marina frowned at the cheerful nurse. Her head throbbed in rhythm to all her aching bruises. "Where are my cats? How did I get here? And where am I, anyway?"

"You're at the General. You were brought here because you had a car accident. Your car's been towed to the garage for repairs. The good news is you don't have any broken bones, just scratches and bruises, and a possible concussion. By the way, no one realized there was a dead dog in your trunk until the garage called to say your car smells. But I'm sure now they've removed the source, that'll clear up quickly."

Mrs. McTavish's dog. Caesar had died. The depressed feeling that had accompanied her as she had left the old woman's house returned with force. "My cats?" she asked, closing her eyes to try to regain perspective.

"Your cats are fine, doctor. They survived the crash with hardly a scratch. The paramedics said they probably saved your life. When the police spotted your smashed up car by the side of the road this morning, the cats were lying on top of you. Their warmth kept you alive. The other veterinarian from your clinic came by to pick up the cats and take them to your home."

Marina's eyes snapped open at that. John knew she was here? Why hadn't he woken her up when he came by?

The nurse's eyes were wide with envy. "Aren't you lucky, working with such a hunk? Is he single?"

Marina nodded her head and then looked away hoping to discourage further conversation on the subject. It always irritated her how women fawned over John Zigley, her new partner. It wasn't as if he were handsome. His hawk-like features weren't balanced and his bedside manner was nothing to brag about. He always seemed to shout at her. Still, that was no reason to be rude to the nurse.

"Guess the accident's got me all jittery." She took a deep breath, which resulted in a fit of coughing, her dry throat closing tighter with each hack.

"Dr. Preston, please, stay calm," the nurse said, fetching a glass of water for her to sip. "You haven't recovered completely from your allergy attack yet."

"What allergy?" Marina asked, wheezing and trying to catch her breath between sips. "I don't have any allergies."

"The doctor suspects the pine needles may have been the cause, they were all over your coat and on the cats' fur. Though I can't imagine where you came across them in this area, but anything's possible, I suppose. Now, was there anything else you wanted to know?"

"No," Marina whispered, her thoughts spinning.

RELEASED with strict instructions to rest and recuperate, she spent the first night at home, cuddling with the cats. John phoned to ask how she was and she told, "Stop worrying, I'm fine. You can't get rid of me that quickly."

His silence worried her.

"What's wrong? I was just kidding."

"Nothing. By the way, sorry about Caesar. Saw that one coming."

"It shouldn't have happened," she said in a hard voice, and then immediately regretted her show of anger.

"We can't tell people how to live their lives, Marina." John's deep voice was steeped in compassion as it came over the phone line. "That dog meant the world to Mrs. McTavish."

If the dog had meant the world to her, why hadn't she asked for more medication, or called Marina sooner for help? But she didn't say any of that aloud. This was hardly the time for a debate. She hung up after promising to rest quietly.

BY MORNING, Marina was determined to start work. Her bruises had turned shades of blue, green, and yellow, but that was hardly a reason to spend the day lazing in bed. So, she and the cats got into the rental car she'd asked to be dropped off for her; and they all drove to work as usual.

Marina entered the clinic with Puddy at her heals. Salisha lingered by the doorway having positioned herself under the safety of a chair. Before the receptionist could ask too many questions, Marina breezed past.

John was in surgery pulling out porcupine quills

from a dog's muzzle. She tried to sneak past him into the kennel area.

Before she'd taken a couple of steps, John's gruff voice stopped her in her tracks. "What the Hell are you doing here?" His voice boomed loud enough to start a howling from the back.

Marina entered the surgery. "I'm fine, thank you very much. And how are you?" Instinctively, she checked on the dog's condition. Luckily, the quills hadn't penetrated far enough into the muzzle to invade the gums.

"Go home." John's concentration stayed on his work.

Ignoring his instructions, Marina headed to the kennel area. She did a quick survey of each patient awaiting treatment. Puddy sniffed every corner of the room, rubbing his scent along the washtub and cabinets. Salisha stuck her head around the doorway and then raced across the open space, pawed open the empty cage at the end and made herself at home. She padded the plush towel laid out for her inside, beside a bowl of water and one with crunchies. Marina shook her head in amusement at her reticent cat and bent down to pet her.

Her hand contacted scaly skin. Startled, she jerked back. The dragon's snout was inches from her face. She scrambled back on hands and knees practically stumbling over her two cats, who raced in opposite directions.

They were in that forest again.

The snout turned to the side, and a golden orb with a vertical pupil peered at her, blinking once. The dragon expelled smoke and she choked on the astringent stench.

She stared at it through watery eyes, unable to believe what she saw. Its snout was at least twice her length. Covered in shiny golden scales that seemed to go on forever, glinted in the morning light. What a terrifying creature! And straight out of legend.

It moved further back, turning its head one way, then another, eyeing her dispassionately. As if satisfied with its inspection, it retreated. The wings spread wide and it stretched its sinewy neck up and let out a bellow that reduced Marina to shudders. Then it swung back down and stared at her with a disconcerting gaze.

Did it expect a reply?

"WHERE have you been?" John said.

She was on the kennel room floor, with Salisha curled on her lap, and Puddy padding at her shins.

"What do you mean?" What had happened? Why was she on the floor?

"You come in here after I specifically told you to go home, then disappear. Your rental car's still outside. The cats are nowhere to be found. Then suddenly, here you all are again. So, where were you?" John looked exasperated.

Marina remained silent, her hand absently stroking Salisha. Had this last visit with the dragon been another hallucination? Had the car accident somehow damaged her psychologically? But then, where had she gone a few minutes ago? And more importantly, where had the cats disappeared to as well?

"What am I going to do with you?" John asked. When she didn't reply, he added, "Marina, I know you're not happy. Are you thinking of leaving?"

Was she? Had she pushed herself too far? Was she having a breakdown? She'd grown tired of life of late and knew she'd been distancing herself from people. Was this breakdown a sign she'd distanced herself so far, she was losing track of reality?

"Marina," he said, "why don't we have dinner tonight and talk this over?"

She looked up at him and nodded. "Yes, I think I might need some time off."

"Time off?" John sounded surprised and then a wide smile spread across his craggy features, like a sunbeam on a cloudy day. "You mean a vacation? Yes. Great idea. I should have thought of it myself."

"Isn't that what we were just talking about?"

"Well," he said, looking sheepish, "I was worried you wanted to leave the practice."

"But I love being a vet." Putting Salisha aside, Marina drew her legs up and rested her forehead on her knees. "I'm just tired of not being able to help."

"Now you're being foolish. You're invaluable to me. Your patients adore you. Is it the McTavish case? There was nothing you could have done for Caesar. He was too far gone. You can't save every animal, Marina. You know that."

She looked up. "It was such a senseless death, John. And lately, there've been so many."

"You're burnt out. A vacation is the best thing. I should have thought of it sooner." He brushed her blonde hair back gently, a finger skirting the bruise on her forehead. "Where are you thinking of going?"

"I don't think I have a choice."

"What do you mean?"

"Nothing." How could she explain about the twin suns to John? He would ask for her resignation. And she loved this job. Working with him. Despite the McTavishes of this world. She wasn't ready to quit or be laid off. Not yet. Was she?

"Look, I'm fine," she said. "Give me a second to get my coat on and we can get to work." She scrambled to her feet and headed for her office.

John bellowed to her to come back.

A dog howled in response.

She ignored both calls and reached for the lab coat behind her office door.

And turned to find herself at the edge of the clearing, the forest behind her, the dragon in front, and her cats at her feet. Instinct urged her to run and Marina was about to obey when the dragon took a step back. Slowly, it lowered its head to the ground, its golden eyes unblinking. She frowned, confused by its docile behavior.

If this were another hallucination, would her heart stop if, in her imagination, the dragon ate her?

Puddy was the first to react. He strode forward and sniffed at the dragon's snout and then to her shock, he licked it. Salisha, smart cat that she was, stayed glued to the back of Marina's trembling legs.

Her instinct to flee warred with her veterinary training that told her this animal was not acting normal for a wild beast, or even an imaginary one.

Puddy, brave hero that he was, seemed to concur. He always licked her patients if he thought them unwell or unhappy. Now the large black and white cat strode around the dragon's snout rubbing his quivering tail on the scales and looking back at her with expectation. She should never have acclimatized her pets to visiting with her patients. What had she been thinking?

If the dragon had meant to eat any of them, Puddy should have already been served up as the appetizer. She gave a sigh of resignation at the plea in both dragon and cat's eyes. Obviously the giant beast wanted something from her. She'd bet her license on it. And since this hallucination didn't seem in the mood to end yet, she stepped forward and then stumbled on her lab coat that she had half shrugged on back at the clinic.

If what she were seeing was real, had the dragon brought her here? Her physical disappearance from the clinic, and the presence of her coat suggested it could have.

Dragons were supposed to be mythical creatures. So, finding her in another planet or dimension, and picking her out of millions of other people and bringing her here should have been a cinch for it. Right? A hysterical laugh burst out at the absurd thought, but a practical explanation was beyond her.

Slowly, she adjusted her coat and advanced, murmuring, "Nice dragon."

The dragon retreated. Each of its steps matched ten of hers. Then it lay on its belly and waited, like a camel in the desert, crouched down so the rider could mount.

Marina stood beside a foreleg that looked more like a pillar than an appendage.

"Well, guys, are you up for this?" she asked the cats.

Puddy scaled the leg as if the question were rhetorical, but Salisha was nowhere in sight. Guessing correctly that the nervous cat would have gone for the nearest large object to hide behind, Marina found her behind the closest tree. Picking her up, she strode back to the dragon. Puddy was already seated majestically on one of the dragon's enormous shoulder blades, patiently waiting for them.

"Think of it as a car ride," she whispered to Salisha.

The cat howled and tried to claw up to her shoulders. Marina held tight, not prepared to lose her here.

"You'll just have to trust me," she told the cat and, tentatively, approached the dragon's foreleg again. With a firm grip on the scales with one hand and holding her terrified cat in the other, she heaved herself upwards. She climbed until she could settle between the dragon's shoulder blades. Puddy came to rest beside her.

Salisha pressed herself into the safety of Marina's arms. Marina hung on tight to the cat and the dragon.

With a few strokes of its powerful wings, they were air-borne, soaring high into the clouds. Marina dug her free hand between the overlapping scales to get a better grip and flattened herself over the two cats. The dragon twisted to catch the wind, wings outstretched. And Salisha's protest howl rang across the land.

They flew over the mountains, passing snow-tipped peaks at great speed until finally they reached a barren, rocky cliff. She swallowed a scream as they headed straight for the walls. Just when she was sure she would never see John or the clinic again, the opening of a giant cave loomed into view.

The dragon casually tucked its wings in a second before they would have collided into the surrounding barrier. Puddy scrambled down and ran into the cave. Vertigo struck Marina so she hastily slid after him, Salisha in her arms. Anything to get away from that ledge.

The light of the afternoon suns dimly penetrated the interior of the lair. A huge green egg sat among a pile of bones that Puddy was investigating. The egg was tilted sideways, partially open on top.

She released Salisha, who raced off to hide in a corner of the cave. Carefully, and hugging the side of the cave walls, Marina approached the egg. As she peered over a cracked end, a jaw snapped at her and she jerked back.

A high-pitched cry assaulted her ears. Hastily she backed up but curiosity got the better of her. Keeping a wide distance from the snapping jaws, she moved around for a closer look. A baby dragon was caught, half in, half out of the egg, one of its wings savagely pierced by the sharp end of a broken shell.

Her first thought was that she should have brought her medical bag. But then, she hadn't planned this trip. The baby needed to be released from that shell. But how? The shell looked as solid as granite slabs. Then she changed her mind. As long as he was trapped, the shell could serve well as a harness while she tended to the torn wing. It was those snapping jaws that were a worry.

Her lab coat! Quickly, she took it off and emptied the pockets. John was forever accusing her of pinching stuff from the treatment rooms, but she was thankful for her kleptomania as she found medical tape, a pair of scissors and a handful of cotton swabs. First, she used the coat to bind those dangerous snapping jaws. Soon, the baby dragon's cries, muffled by the coat, echoed inside the cave as Marina carefully worked to release the injured wing.

Puddy, having satisfied his curiosity with all the smells and tastes inside the cave, strolled over to sit at the entrance with the mother dragon and watch Marina work. No sign of Salisha. She'd worry about her when this job was done. The one thing she was certain of was that Salisha always found a safe place to roost no matter where her owner took her.

Marina turned her attention back to her patient and went in search of a slender bone fragment from the many littering the floor, no doubt from the dragon's previous meals. Finding one of a satisfactory length and width, she fashioned it into a needle. Then tearing threads from her shirt, she set to patching up the torn wing.

The light was suddenly obscured. The mother dragon loomed over her, peering intently at Marina's handiwork. In the dark, for just a moment, the dragon looked a lot like the way Mrs. McTavish had, while watching Marina tend to Caesar. She blinked rapidly, dispelling the image and resumed her work, impatiently waving the mother dragon away.

By the time she was finished, it was late afternoon. Puddy was fast asleep and Salisha had come out of hiding to explore the cave.

The mother dragon sat quietly on the ledge observing her. Marina moved away from the egg and went to sit by the ledge opening, no longer concerned about the height. She leaned her tired head against the cliff wall and tried to ignore the baby dragon's cries. In time, it was easier, for he grew tired and quieter until he finally slept, snoring softly.

At dusk, she got up, and with the mother dragon's help, cracked the hard shell, gently releasing the baby from the egg. They worked quietly, trying not to wake up the patient. Sleep would help heal more than anything else she could do. The muzzle was left to the last. Finally, she untied even that. Starting to feel a little chilly, she absently shrugged the coat back on.

The baby stirred restlessly, but was too exhausted to waken. In the morning, the mother dragon would be able to start feeding her baby.

Marina turned to look at the mother dragon, hoping in some way to communicate that her work here was done. The dragon was again on its belly, watching her, and waiting.

Marina hesitated, glancing around. The cats were sleeping off their meal, having had lots to eat in the dark corners of cave filled with leftover dragon feed.

Marina found this world strangely compelling. The urge to see what the next day would bring was as strong as the urge to go exploring in those woods she'd first landed in. What animals lived here, besides the dragons?

Unlike at home, she felt of use here. True, she didn't have any medication or equipment to practice her profession. Though she'd done well enough with the baby. She peered around the cave, searching for an answer. Would life here be any better than at home?

Stepping up to the entrance, Marina looked toward the horizon. The two suns were setting, hidden behind a haze that turned their orange rays crimson. Here, she may never need to deal with humans again.

Suddenly, Mrs. McTavish came to mind. Staring into the dragon's eyes, Marina recalled the soulful looks that Caesar had given his mistress, the tender stroke of the paw to gain her attention, the wag of his tail whenever she came into the room.

For all his skipped medication and matted fur, Caesar had adored his mistress. And the dog must have meant the world to the old woman. For even if she couldn't afford the medication he'd needed, according to her daughter, Mrs. McTavish had given up buying her own food to feed him.

The dragon stared at her solemnly. Then the two cats woke up and stretched. Puddy came over to rub along Marina's leg, and looked up at her expectantly. Salisha too was staring at her, but with a calm look of acceptance of this new world she'd been dropped into. And it occurred to Marina that she and Salisha had a lot in common. Neither liked surprises. And both liked to have control over their surroundings. But with enough time to find acceptance, like Puddy, they were both capable of handling any challenge put before them with grace.

Marina knew then exactly what she wanted to do. What she must do to make peace with herself. Or no world, this or the other, would ever be palatable to her.

With a last look at the wildness of this place, she picked up Salisha and climbed onto the mother dragon's back. Puddy scaled up on his own and found the best position for viewing their ascent.

Before she could say they were ready, the dragon swooped down from the ledge, leaving Marina breathless until the wings caught the wind and they soared up and across the sky.

She awoke at her desk at the clinic, head resting on her arms, the cats snuggled up on either side of her. Her chair squeaked when she leaned back. Gently, she stroked Salisha and Puddy.

"Are we back for good this time?" she asked them.

They didn't reply, but a chair slammed against the wall in the office next door and footsteps hurried toward her. John came to a halt by the doorway. He was in jeans and a checked shirt. His hair was ruffled. She saw then why that nurse and every other woman who met him found him so appealing.

She tilted her head, feeling a teasing light flicker inside her. "Something wrong, John?"

"You're back. Staying long? Or should I look for a new partner? If you don't care about me or the clinic, why did you offer to become my partner?"

"John," Marina said, interrupting his flow of words. She'd never heard him sound this down before. She got up and went around the desk toward him. "You were worried."

"Damn straight I was worried. Where the Hell have you all been? Shit, I sound like a broken record. And what happened to your lab coat? I've half a mind to dock your pay."

Marina looked down in surprise and then took off the offending coat that was ripped and tattered in several places by the baby's attempts to free himself.

"It's a long story."

Hunger pangs were gnawing at her stomach. The cats might have eaten while they were away, but she hadn't, not in a long while. "Are we going out for dinner? You know, to talk over my vacation plans?"

He stared at her, looked out the window, then at her again, eyebrow raised in question.

Only then did she notice a reddish haze on the sky, hinting at the coming dawn. She'd lost track of time. She smiled at John. "How about breakfast then?"

"What's the matter with you?" John's raised voice sounded exasperated.

Why did he always shout at her? She was sure he

didn't do it to everyone else. He had obviously not done it with that nurse.

"You disappear for hours on end and all you can think of is food?" he asked.

"But I haven't eaten all day. I'm hungry."

John folded his arms. "What am I going to do with you, Marina? All right, you can come over to my place. I'll make you eggs. But you can't bring those cats. They stay in the kennel here. Brutus doesn't like cats."

"Told you it was a bad idea to get a Rottweiler for a pup," she said. "We can lock him in the bathroom and then he won't be any trouble to my cats."

"We are not locking up my dog!"

"John, you're shouting at me."

"You never listen to me. Talking to you is like talking to a post."

Salisha and Puddy followed them out to the car park. "Shall we take your van or my rental?" she asked.

"Mine." He slid the door open. The cats immediately jumped in and he scowled at them.

Marina hesitated, and then headed back to the clinic.

"Where are you going now?" he asked.

"I'll be right back, I forgot something."

She ran to her office and grabbed her medical bag. When she got into the van, she tossed it into the back. She gave him a cheerful smile as she buckled herself into the passenger seat, for suddenly everything about life felt as if it were just perfect, including going to John's place for breakfast at the break of dawn.

"Are you ever going to tell me where you disappeared to?" he asked, giving her a side-glance.

"I'd rather we talk about my vacation plans."

"Thought of someplace fun, did you?" He grinned too, as if catching her good humor. "I wouldn't mind a vacation myself." He gave her another look, and this one had a definite gleam that suggested he had more then sun tanning and swimming in mind. Marina felt herself warm up.

"Want to go together?" he asked, ultra casual.

DRAGON DREAMS

"Maybe head out to Hawaii? We could hire someone to fill in at the clinic." He glanced out the driver's side window. "Or are you tired of me already?" he asked softly.

Hawaii was not what she had in mind when she mentioned vacation. How would he react to her plans? She could certainly use his help. "I thought of taking a few days off to paint Mrs. McTavish's house," she said in a quiet voice, glancing at him hesitantly. At his silence, she frowned. Was he disappointed that she wasn't going to a sunny location? Could he understand what she needed to do, and why?

"You're pretty good with a hammer," she suggested with an encouraging smile. "And her roof leaks."

John frowned at her and then he nodded, as if he did indeed understand. "I'd like to help." His smile was breathtaking.

Marine reached over and kissed his cheek, surprising both of them. "Thanks for being patient with me."

He took her hand and kissed the back of it. He kept hold of it he drove, ignoring Salisha's howl from the back seat as he took a sharp corner. His thumb gently rubbed across her palm, sending tingles up her arm. "I'm glad you're including me in this." He sounded as if she'd given him a birthday present.

"Well," Marina said, trying to hide her mischievous laughter, "since Mrs. McTavish just lost Caesar, I also hoped we could get her another pet."

"We?" he said in a worried tone. The circling motion on her palm stopped.

"Hmm. I was thinking along the lines of a little Rottweiler pup."

He flung her hand away. "You are not giving away my dog!"

"You're shouting again. If you keep this up, I won't tell you about the wonderful place I just visited."

They were almost at his apartment when something large and sharp scraped along the top of the van.

He swerved off the road and checked to see what he'd hit.

Marina dived to the back of the van.

She knew he'd find nothing on the road that could

have harmed his van. Any more than she had when the same thing had happened to her Fiat on Marina's way to Mrs. McTavish's house. At her chuckle, he whipped around to look at her.

She hugged her medical bag and gave him wide smile.

"What're you doing?" he asked.

"Learning to be prepared," she replied.

The author tells us that she has worked as an Animal Health Technician in both small- and large-animal hospitals for several years.

DRAGON DREAMS

CAT CALL

by K.D. Wentworth

I SAW THE BODY the moment I squeezed back into the living room through my catdoor. It was male and overweight, dressed in frayed jeans and a red shirt, both of which smelled much more intriguing than anything my tidy roommate Sidley would ever have worn. The hands, large and bloodied, were clutched into fists. The brown eyes stared sightlessly up at the ceiling. The aromatic tang of blood lingered in the air, and the house was still as a cornered mouse.

How very odd. I curled my tail around my gray and white hindquarters, my best thinking position, and gave my whiskers a thorough wash. I'd never seen a dead human before and this one was most unexpected, sprawled across the worn roses of our living room carpet. When Sidley left this morning, the most I'd hoped was that he'd bring home a dead bird or two. A kill of this magnitude was impressive.

Of course, I, Hudson, (named for Sidley's ex-father-in-law, not a warm relationship, I've been given to understand), have been totally mystified anyway ever since this crazy business concerning *birds* started a few weeks ago. Herm Sidley and I have lived together in this humble abode for three years now, and he's never before evidenced the slightest interest in birds. In fact, months passed after I moved in before he could even bring himself to touch *me,* so I can't imagine what prompted him taking up this silliness he calls "bird-watching."

It's understood, of course, that cats watch birds. I keep a careful eye on the robins and sparrows outside Sidley's bungalow. They're certainly more interesting than that pointless box Sidley stares at all evening. But cats do more than gaze wistfully up at the trees; *we* do our very best to bring one of the saucy creatures down from time to time, and I thought from the first Sidley didn't have it in him. It's not his fault, though. Feline companionship and example came into his life late.

Whenever this so-called "bird-watching" was to take place, a woman would arrive at our house, not a good sign with Sidley. When females are about, he turns red, stammers, and stares at the floor, never taking advantage of the opportunity to stretch and show himself off to his best advantage.

This particular she was thin as a post and had the intent, lean-bellied look of a cat about to pounce on something delicious. She had dreary yellow fur on her head and darted about the living room, chattering louder than an angry sparrow. Even worse, she always reeked of flowers as though she'd been out rolling in the garden. I found it an overwhelming and noxious scent, quite unlike the delicate bouquet of freshly slaughtered mouse.

AFTER HER arrival, the subsequent sequence of events was always the same. She would natter on about the differences between "pileated woodpeckers" and "nuthatches" (as though they don't all taste the same), raise the window shade as if she were looking for something, then haul Sidley off to view "our fine feathered friends."

The strangest part is that minutes later the front door would always open again. Strangers would come prowling in as though they belonged there, peer out the windows, use the phone (which is quite indiscriminating and will talk to absolutely anyone). If I so much as poked my nose out from behind the couch, they threw magazines at me. Sooner or later, the faithless phone would ring. They would answer, then leave a few minutes before Sidley returned, a thoroughly mystifying chain of events.

This morning had begun like all the others involving the detested "Marie." It was a cloud-ridden, damp day, not the sort at all for stalking birds, I would have thought. Marie bounced in the door and cooed at me, though I wouldn't let her get within half a room. As always, that made her giggle as if being despised were amusing. Anxious to avoid the inevitable invading strangers, I exited via my cat door to do some bird-watching of my own, hopefully of a more productive nature than Sidley's. He never brought home anything from these outings but a stupid smile.

When the sun was overhead, I returned, feeling peckish and thinking Sidley would probably be back by now and I could wheedle a bit of milk. Instead, I found the house empty —

— except for the body sprawled across the threadbare carpet in the living room.

Now, usually there's nothing I'd rather roll on than a newly dead body. Mouse bodies, squirrel bodies, rabbit bodies, bird bodies, they're all delightful, but this human corpse was a bit overwhelming. I decided to nap instead.

Sometime later, the front door creaked open. "What the — !"

I bolted up, eyes expectant.

"My God, Hudson!" Sidley looked as though he might keel over.

Hunger, no doubt. I knew exactly how he felt.

Disturbed dust motes danced in the light slanting in through the open front door. "There's blood all over the living room!" he said.

I cocked my head. Trust Sidley to state the obvious.

"How — ?" He froze in place, one hand to his chest, his mouth hanging open in that unappealing way only he has truly mastered.

I positioned myself between him and the corpse, pricked my ears at a meaningful angle. *You can pour me a nice stiff bowl of milk, while you're trying to figure it out,* I thought helpfully.

"It's Bill Vincent, from next door!" He glanced down at me, his eyes as startled as a just-flushed rabbit's. "Did you — ?"

Oh, right, I thought, *like I'm going to bring down something that big on an empty stomach.* I arched my back and loosed a low growling complaint, to let him know that milk — now — would be a very good idea.

Sidley collapsed into his green armchair and lowered his head into his trembling hands. "No, of course not," he muttered. "It had to be someone else. Hudson isn't vicious."

If I don't see some milk real soon, buster, I thought, *you may have reason to reconsider!*

"The police," Sidley said. He fumbled for the phone beside his chair. "We have to call the police. Don't touch anything!

Hadn't planned to. I leaped onto the arm of his chair.

Before he could dial, though, a siren wailed outside. Car doors slammed. Sidley hung up and opened the door.

A hulking policeman stood on our porch. "We had a call about a murder."

"Thank goodness you're here, officer!" Sidley said.

The policeman stepped inside, smelling of onions and garlic, intriguing, but not at all appealing.

"It's this — this body!" Sidley pointed with a trembling finger.

"I see." The policeman's lined face fell into concerned folds, but he kept a hand near the holster on his belt. "Do you know this person?"

Sidley nodded, then blurted out the whole bird-watching story, finishing with his discovery of the corpse. I lashed my tail with disapproval. Even I found the tale ridiculous, and I had witnessed most of it for myself.

The policeman, whose name was Officer Rogers, scribbled determinedly in a battered little notebook.

"Will you call the young lady and have her drop over, sir? We'd like to take her statement and back up your alibi."

Sidley swallowed hard and admitted he didn't have her phone number. He'd met Marie at the park four weeks ago and she'd always insisted upon calling him whenever they got together. She had an unlisted number and her mother didn't allow her to give it out.

"I see." Officer Rogers' mouth quirked knowingly and he bent over his notebook. Sirens howled and then more police arrived.

Men and women streamed inside the small living room. Lights flashed until I was half-blind. People crawled over the rug like mice, picking up tiny bits of who-knows-what and stowing them in plastic bags.

Frankly, this was not how I'd envisioned spending the afternoon. My stomach grew ever emptier, my temper more foul.

One of the other policemen handed Officer Rogers a long thin metallic shape with one end encased in clear plastic. He held it up to the light and squinted. "Have you ever seen this before, Mr. Sidley?"

Sidley took the bag and the plastic crinkled as he turned it over. "It looks like one of my screwdrivers."

Rogers took it back. "This was lying beneath the victim and matches a five inch puncture in his back. I think we'd better read you your rights."

Sidley picked me up and clutched me against his chest in a convulsive gesture of despair. We are not a touchy-feelie pair, so I knew matters were grim. I laid my ears back, but otherwise endured until the officer made him put me down so he could apply handcuffs.

Yeah, I thought sourly, *you wimps better look out for old.*

Sidley. It's obvious he could whip his weight in arthritic rabbits.

They hauled both Sidley and the untidy body away, then searched the house from top to bottom, pulling out all the drawers, checking for loose floorboards. They made so much racket, I was tempted to vacate again. Living with Sidley isn't rewarding enough to put up with that sort of nonsense. Finally, they strung long yellow tape across all the doors, except mine, and departed.

The prospect of milk vanished, I settled in for a long, hungry afternoon. Outside, the stupid birds carried on with no one to teach them discretion.

SIDLEY RETURNED that night, "out on bail," and more distraught than ever. He'd been forced to put up the deed to his rundown bungalow in order to spring himself and now paced the worn floorboards of the living room. They creaked at every other step. "I don't care if Vincent did live next door," he said. "I had no reason to kill him. We'd barely spoken since he moved in!"

He lurched to a halt in the middle of the floor and we both studied the brownish-red stain. The aroma of blood lingered, more interesting to me, I was fairly certain, than to Sidley, who's never shown the least capacity to appreciate the finer things in life.

"I'm not supposed to be in here," he said finally. "No one is — it's an official crime scene. But how else am I going to figure out what happened? And besides, I have nowhere else to go."

Well, you could go to the fridge, I thought helpfully, then nudged his leg with my nose. It was sheer practicality, of course. I always think best on a full stomach.

Sidley tottered into the kitchen and opened the refrigerator. I paced back and forth, rubbing against his pants legs. "Obviously, she wanted me out of the house," Sidley said as he poured milk into my bowl. "But why? Whoever killed Vincent could have done it anywhere, unless they specifically wanted to implicate me."

I lapped the milk, thinking. Each time after Sidley left, the invading strangers used the phone. Then later the phone would ring and they answered it. So — it was obvious! To find out what was going on, Sidley should make the phone tell what it knew. It was a dreadful device, capable of the most earsplitting clamor, and I wouldn't have been surprised if it was behind the whole mess. I couldn't imagine why Sidley put up with the cheeky thing in the first place, the way it rang whenever it felt like it, taking his mind off me at the most inopportune moments.

I darted into the living room, leaped onto Sidley's chair, which was beside the telephone, and yowled.

"Shhh!" Sidley grabbed at me. "Hudson, I'm not supposed to be here! No one is! If you're not quiet, someone will call the police again, and this time they won't let me out on bail!"

I slithered out of reach, still yowling. Sometimes Sidley can be so dense. *The phone, idiot!* I thought at him. *Pick up the stupid phone and make it tell what's been going on in here!*

He skirted the chair, attempting to corner me against the end table. I straddled the phone, arched my back, and raked his unprotected hand with bared claws on his next try. *Not me! The phone!*

He leaped back, hand in his mouth. "Hud-thon!" he said indistinctly around the injured flesh. I nudged the black handset off its stand with my nose and then gazed at it meaningfully with blazing green eyes. The hard plastic shape clattered to the floor and dangled on its curly cord.

Sidley extracted his bleeding hand from his mouth and wrapped it in a handkerchief. "Are you saying the killer might have used the phone?" The springs creaked as he sank down in the chair. "The last number I called was Official Time this morning in order to set my watch, so if I hit the redial button and get a different number, it would be someone the killer called!"

The phone started making those nasty off-the-hook noises that always set my fur on edge. I arched my back and spit at it, so he hastily depressed the biggest button, then pushed one of the smaller ones. The phone sang one of its silly little songs.

"Hello?" Sidley said. "Marie?" His straggly eyebrows rose expressively. "What do you mean — how did I get this number? Someone dialed it from my phone this morning, either before or after they murdered my neighbor in my living room with my own screwdriver!" He flinched, then stared at the handset and shook his head. "She hung up, Hudson. I don't suppose I should be surprised."

HEY, don't underestimate yourself, old son, I thought, then curled up, tail to nose, to catnap on the arm of his easy chair.

I was awakened later by a stealthy knock at the front door. I stretched. Not the police, I supposed, since, on those lame television shows Sidley was so fond of, they rarely bothered with proprieties at the homes of suspected murderers.

Sidley, also dozing in the chair, stiffened. "Wha—?"

Ever the poet, I thought, then trotted to the door to investigate. The traitorous she, Marie, was on the front porch. I detected her particularly noxious reek of squished flowers at once.

"Herm?" she whispered, her voice as smooth as a cat slinking after a robin. "It's me, Marie. Let me in! I want to explain!"

Sidley stumbled up out of the chair. "Explain it to the police!" He snatched up the phone and punched in three quick numbers.

I gazed back over my shoulder at him. He sounded almost forceful, an altogether different sort of Sidley. How unusual.

The lock rattled, then the front door swung inward. Marie ducked under the yellow tape into the living room. She had a key in one hand and a small, but efficient looking gun in the other. "Hang up the phone, Herm. It's too late for dramatics."

"Oh, I suppose you've come here to admit this morning had more to do with dead bodies than yellow-bellied sapsuckers!"

I laid my ears back as she snatched the phone out of his hand, then slammed it back into its cradle. "Cut the act, Herm. Uncle Emilio knows you're a federal agent," she said coolly.

"*Me?*"

"Yes, *you,*" she said. "Face it. Nobody could be as clueless as you pretend to be."

Sidley sank back into his easy chair.

"You did have us fooled at first," she said, "but now

we're wise to your act. It's time to put our cards on the table. That snake Bert Visotti won't be singing to the feds about Uncle Emilio's business anymore, and you're going to take the fall, unless . . ."

Sidley glanced at the phone, then turned his gaze deliberately aside. His fingers trembled. "Unless?"

"Unless you join the family."

Sidley was beyond words at this point. I darted up and sat in his lap with my ears flattened. *He doesn't need another family,* I thought crossly. *He has me.*

"I mean, think about it," Marie went on. "You've made being boring into a fine art. We could send you anywhere, use you to get any sort of information, and no one would ever suspect a thing. *We* certainly wouldn't have, when the feds moved Cousin Bert next door, except you were just too perfect. Nobody can be that bland. You're going to have to lighten up a little."

Two bright spots of red bloomed in Sidley's colorless cheeks. "Really?" he said in a strained voice. His fingers crept toward the phone. "I hadn't realized I'd overplayed my hand that badly."

The stupid phone doesn't know anything else, I thought. *Let's jump her together and scratch her eyes out.*

Sidley's fingers groped. The phone teetered in its cradle, then fell off. He froze and we all three stared. In another second or two, it was going to make those awful off-the-hook noises that always made me want to leap out of my fur. I yowled low in my throat.

"Hang it up, Herm!" Marie was insistent.

"No," Sidley said quietly. "Hang it up yourself."

Someone hang it up! I thought, lashing my tail with anticipated displeasure, but then it was too late. The phone went into its loathsome act, wailing at a pitch that threatened to make my ears bleed. They both ignored it.

"If you won't join us," Marie said, "Uncle Emilio's instructions are to kill you."

"Go ahead," Sidley said. He was pale and rigid and seemed somehow taller than usual. "And then see if you can get one of my other neighbors to take the blame for *that*. Of course, two killings in the same house might look even more suspicious."

The phone went on caterwauling and I joined in, running back and forth on top of the chair. *Make it stop!* I thought angrily at Sidley.

"Oh, I don't know," Marie said. "Remorse and all that. Perhaps you came back to the scene of the crime and then killed yourself out of guilt."

If neither one of them would shut up that stupid phone, then it was up to me. Otherwise, my brains were going to boil inside my skull and Marie might as well use the gun to put us both out of our misery.

I leaped from the back of the chair and knocked the phone off onto the floor. It kept screeching anyway, so I leaped down and bit its hard plastic head while I tried to disembowel its button-studded belly with my hind claws. I heard a click, then a three note song.

"Get away from that phone!" Marie's voice held a new, frantic note. The living room exploded and something raked me with bared claws. Through a hot red veil, I dimly heard Sidley yelling, Marie screeching. I tried to bite my mysterious attacker, but my teeth closed only on air.

My side throbbed as though a raging Airdale had thrown me against a wall. I tried to lift my head to sniff the injury and failed. Whatever was going on, I thought groggily, I was not going to like it.

"He'll be all right, Mr. Sidley," someone was saying in an aggravatingly cheerful voice.

The air had a familiar reek — metal and plastic and antiseptic. The vet's office! I yowled weakly in disgust. How unfair! It was not even close to shot or fleabath time.

"It's nothing to worry about, hardly more than a flesh wound," the voice said blithely, though I bet she would have felt differently if it had been *her* flesh. "I'll be able to take the stitches out in a few days."

"Can I leave him for a couple of hours?" Sidley asked. "I talked the police into bringing me here first, but I have to go down to the station and clear

CAT CALL

up the details. They've got a squad car waiting out front."

No! I managed to open my eyes. The room raced around in sickening circles as though it'd sniffed too much catnip. *Don't leave me at the vet's, you idiot!*

"Of course you can." The vet reached down to stroke behind my ears and I was too weak to sink my teeth into her hand as she deserved. "Hudson is a hero. He was absolutely brilliant, hitting Redial to call 911 and summon the police. And don't worry about the bill. There won't be any charges. It's the least I can do for such a clever, brave cat."

"That's very, um, k-kind of you," Sidley managed, as always, awkward as a six-month-old kitten in the presence of a mateable female. "Perhaps I could repay your kindness to Hudson by t-taking you out to dinner, or —" He looked away and bit his lip. "I don't suppose you like bird-watching?"

No! I thought at him in desperation. *This is not the time to finally find your nerve!*

"Why, I love bird-watching." Her face went the most amazing shade of pink as though no one had ever asked her to do something that stupid and boring in her entire life. "When would you like to go?"

I laid my head between my paws and sighed.

So, that's all the thanks a cat gets for saving the day, six stitches along the ribcage that preclude any serious attempts at stalking junebugs and subsequent invasions of my home by the vet without warning. I will say that she leaves the wretched needles behind when she visits, and, much to my surprise, she does know exactly where a cat likes to be scratched, not that I ever let on when she's hit that certain spot.

Now, if she could just teach Sidley how to bring home a dead bird from time to time, I might be willing to reconsider my position on this matter. And who knows? Stranger things have happened.   ❧

The author tells us, "I wrote 'Cat Call' as a follow-up

to a story titled 'Cat and Mouse' published in Crafty Cat Crimes *a few years back, also featuring Hudson and Sidley. Although I cohabit with 167 pounds of dog at the moment (Akita + Siberian Hussy — I mean Huskey), I was once owned by a large grey cat who decided he would live with me, whether I wanted him to move in or not. His name was Hudson and we did very well together.*

CAT CALL

A CHRISTMAS CAROL

by Jack Williamson

The day had been great until Janice called. Christmas had always been special, though it was different now. She loved to remember the old days when the whole family got together at Aunt Miranda's. The big dinner, with turkey and ham and Cousin Julia's mincemeat pies, was always on Christmas Eve. The gifts were waiting under the tree, to be opened before breakfast next morning.

She and Bella used to sleep on bed rolls in the attic. Or not sleep, really. They lay awake all night, giggling about gifts they wanted and gifts they were giving and the happy times and funny things remembered from years before. They crept down at dawn to shake the packages and look at the labels and try to guess what was in them.

All that was long ago. She was housebound since the accident, and money was short with Harry gone. Gifts were a problem, but she had been an art teacher and she had done little watercolors for everybody who would be there. Sketches of the big old house and the old elm beside it. She had put Aunt Miranda in the swing, with Uncle Abner pushing her and laughing. She had the little pictures wrapped in gold paper with red ribbons, waiting till Joe came by in his new Lincoln to pick her up for the dinner.

She wanted her own little place to be neat for the holiday just in case anybody came to see her, though these days very few did. She'd scrubbed and swept and dusted, and set the crystal angel to shine in the window. A cat meowed at her when she opened the front door to sweep the step. She hated cats because Harry had been allergic to them. She swatted at it with the broom, but it didn't run.

"Happy holidays, Mrs. Maupin!"

Mr. Anderson called across the street, laughing at her. He was the postman, a plump hearty red-faced man who might have put on a red suit to be a Santa at the mall. She had known him since last Christmas, when he knocked on the door to deliver the box of peanut brittle from Aunt Miranda.

He knew who she was from the address on the box, and he had known Harry at the lodge. He told her his name and said Harry had been a fine and honest gentleman. That had been Harry's birthday. Thinking of him, she had baked a pan of the chocolate pecan cookies he loved. Mr. Anderson said he was on a diet, but she made him take a cookie.

The house was spotless before Janice called.

"Merry Christmas, Molly!" Her voice was shrill and high, not merry at all today. "If Aunt Miranda didn't tell you, she's had to cancel her Christmas dinner."

That felt like a jab in the stomach. She gulped and gripped the phone.

"She hates to disappoint everybody," Janice went on, "but it's her daughter Dawn. The one in Cleveland. She slipped on the ice and broke her hip. It's fixed with pins. The doctors say she'll be okay, but Aunty has to be there with her now."

"I'm sorry," she whispered. "I'll pray for them."

"We're all sorry." Janice waited for a moment and asked, "Molly, are you okay?"

"I'm fine," she said. "I'll be fine."

She hung up the phone and limped to the old rocking chair that had belonged to Harry's mother. She sat there, thinking of all the past Christmas times when the family was larger, twenty people at the long table in the dining room and the kids around bridge table in the den. Uncle Abner carved the huge turkey, and Aunt Miranda let Joe serve big brown mugs of hot buttered rum, though she wouldn't touch it herself.

With so many gone now, or busy with new families of her own, there were only seven now, seven of her little gold-wrapped gifts wrapped and waiting on the kitchen counter for Joe to pick them up. He wouldn't be coming now. She had to gulp at a lump in her throat when she counted them, but she was learning to look at the bright side. Painting them had brought back all the good Christmas times she remembered. Everybody loved the big old house. They would have liked the pictures.

She was still there in the chair when the doorbell rang.

"A package for you, Mrs. Maupin." It was Mr. Anderson, working his way back on her side of the street. "I guess old Santa did remember."

She thanked him, but he wouldn't take another cookie. The package was only the bottle of vitamins she had ordered from AARP. While she was trying to open it, she heard a hungry meow. The yellow-striped cat she had seen on the step. It had slipped inside with Mr. Anderson.

She opened the door again and tried to scat it. It ran and hid behind the sofa. She scatted it again and slapped the sofa with the fly swatter, but it wouldn't come out. Slow and awkward on the walker, she had to give up the chase. She shut the door again and sat back in the rocker, looking at her little stack of gifts.

Maybe she could get Joe to mail them, if she could find brown paper for a stronger wrapping and stamps enough, but they would be too late to matter. She sighed. After all, her life had been good. She was learning to take things as they came. It always made her happy to think of Harry and all they fine times they'd had together.

They'd met in high school. He'd been tall, with golden freckles and curly red hair, a star on the basketball team. She cried when he didn't ask her to the prom, and laughed when he stammered in the way he had then and told her that he'd been too shy. She did miss him terribly, but then all they'd had nearly forty great years together.

She was dozing in the rocker when she heard the cat again. She didn't want it in the house but it was friendly now, purring and rubbing against her legs. It reminded her of the yellow kitten with a red ribbon around its neck that Bella tried to give her on her fifth birthday. Her mother wouldn't let her keep it, because cats were too much trouble. She'd cried when her father took it away.

Sitting there with the cat at her feet, dozing away again, she thought she heard the doorbell. She thought it was Mr. Anderson, though now he was dressed in red and white and fat as a Santa Claus.

"Well, well, Molly Dolly." He boomed at her in Harry's hearty voice. That had been Harry's pet name for her. "Why don't you keep the yellow kitten? It won't hurt me now, and it's as lonely as you are."

The cat woke her, mewing at her feet. It looked hungry. She found a saucer and filled it with the half-and-half she'd saved for her breakfast cereal. Back in the chair she watched it lick the saucer clean. She must have dozed again. The next she knew it was curled up in her lap.

She winked the sleep out of her eyes and stroked its silky yellow fur. It was happy, soft and warm, purring softly, glad to be in the house and full of the rich cream. She forgot the undelivered gifts. She was no longer alone. ❦

THE EYES OF RA

by Jim C. Hines

JACKAL, hawk, baboon, and man gazed with disapproval at what Peshet was about to attempt. The glazed features of the canopic jars flickered with red light from the oil lamp. But the handcrafted jars were as lifeless as the sarcophagus that dominated the tomb. The jars contained Wahankh's organs, but not his *ka*. That had escaped hours ago through the narrow tunnels that angled out from the top of the tomb.

"I do this for Wahankh," she said, trying to answer her unblinking accusers. The poison in her blood made her voice rasp, and the stone walls swallowed her words into silence. "Wahankh and his daughter, Ruia, sister of my heart. May Bast protect her if I can not."

The only response came from the cat curled up in the far corner, who yawned. The brown desert cat had slipped in through the eastern *ka* tunnel shortly after the tomb was sealed. He watched through half-lidded eyes as she turned the beeswax candle, thickening the lines of the sarcophagus drawing that was the hieroglyph for *death*.

"Did Bast send you to chastise me, Bast-ta-sherit?" Bast-ta-sherit . . . *Little Bast*. It would be out of character for the cat-headed Netjert to punish such an unimportant person as herself. Was he here to watch over Wahankh's body or to escort Peshet into death?

So far, the cat had done nothing but hiss and retreat to the corner. She hoped he would remain there. If he damaged the circle . . . the thought sent a tremor through her body.

She had taken most of the afternoon to prepare the circle. "The twin pillars of magic are patience and care," she quoted quietly. So she examined it again, tracing the wax lines to be certain each hieroglyph was properly drawn. Even Wahankh would be pleased with the quality of this work.

She unclasped the golden badge from her hair and placed it in the center of the circle. A dark eye of green and gold, gleamed in the light.

"It was a gift from Wahankh. You would have liked him, Bast-ta-sherit. He was a kind man."

The cat flicked his ears and continued to watch.

Her eyes watered as she recalled the first time she had encountered that badge. Wahankh had been wearing it the day he brought a damaged scroll into the shop of her master, Hapu.

Peshet had been busy rubbing criss-crossed layers of papyrus with a polished shell until they merged into one smooth sheet. Making papyrus was her first duty, and as a result, her hands always smelled like crushed plants.

She had worked for Hapu for as long as she could remember. Her mother had died in childbirth, and Hapu took her in after a runaway horse trampled her father.

Hapu was a good man, but he treated Peshet like a worker. There was no warmth in her world.

Peshet glanced up as Wahankh and Hapu brought the damaged scroll into the back room. Being young and impertinent, she interrupted to ask, "How did such holy writings come to be burned?"

"Attend your duties," Hapu snapped. But Wahankh smiled and knelt so they were at eye level. "How do you know these writings were holy, child?"

THE EYES OF RA

"I saw the invocation to the Netjeru." She pointed to the figures in the far column.

"You can read the hieroglyphs?"

"Only some." She saw that Wahankh was waiting for her to elaborate. "I study the scrolls when there's nothing else to do."

Hapu's jaw dropped, but Wahankh ignored him. "Do you read Hieratic?"

She nodded. "And some Demotic, but that's harder."

She was growing frightened. Had she done something forbidden? Would Hapu punish her? Who was this man with such dark eyes that reached down to the center of her *ka*?

Wahankh laughed in delight. "Child, you are a marvel." He grabbed a golden badge clamped to his hair and showed it to her. "Do you recognize this?"

She bit her lip and looked at Hapu. The air was tense, and she feared saying the wrong thing. "You may answer," he said.

The sharp, slitted eye of the serpent watched her closely. "It's the eye of Sitma-at." She looked away, trying to escape that narrow gaze.

Wahankh laughed again. "Hapu my friend, how did you come to have such a treasure in your home?"

It was months before she realized Wahankh had been referring to *her*.

"I MUST concentrate," Peshet said, blinking back tears at the memory. She chewed on her knuckles, trying not to think about how unprepared she felt. It took years of study to unite the nine facets of her being into a single channel through which the magic could flow. But the time for lessons was over, and she would not see her teacher again in this life.

She took a deep breath, and the poison sent needles through her stomach. The pain brought to mind Jarha, the man who had poisoned her, and a newfound rage helped her focus. She began the incantation with a chant to Osiris. This spell intruded upon his realm as the Netjer of death, and she asked for understanding. As her voice grew soft, the dim light of the tomb began to fade into darkness.

The red of blood filled the edges of her vision. Her body stiffened, and her muscles tightened like ropes under strain. Magic flayed her flesh, hooking into her soul and tugging like an enraged dog. Salty sweat stung her cracked lips. Her throat burned as she repeated the prayer, begging for release.

Her *ka* tore free from her body. She found herself standing on the west bank of the Nile, staring down at the unimposing tomb. A few days ago, it had been nothing more than a bare patch of land. But money worked miracles, and Jarha had been eager to see Wahankh gone from this world.

The thought of Jarha drew her gaze inward, toward the city. To Jarha, Wahankh's death was a chance to seize his land, his wealth . . . and his daughter.

"You have murdered me," whispered Peshet. "You will *not* take Ruia."

Pshet's *ka* entered the house through the central air shaft. It looked unchanged, and she wanted to weep at the brief mirage of normalcy. Oil lamps illuminated the red, mud-brick walls. Small, ceramic statues stood in the corners of the room, each one a token of respect to the Netjeru.

The room was empty. *Of course. Only a buffoon attempts a seduction in the dry, drafty air of the central room.* Jarha was many things, but he was no fool.

She probed the back of the house, stopping to glance wistfully into the library. Her desk was as she had left it. Pots of colored inks held a large sheet of papyrus in place. She had barely finished the first hieroglyph. A brown stain covered the lower half of the page. Ruia's screams had startled her into spilling a pot, destroying an hour's work in an eyeblink.

It took a strong act of will to break away from the library, but she had no time to lose herself in memories. As she moved down the hallway, she heard the faint sound of weeping.

She found them in Wahankh's bedroom. Ruia sat on the edge of the sleeping mat, hands clutched together as she rocked back and forth. Her tears had smeared her eye make-up, tracing black river-beds of kohl down her round cheeks. Her hair — her real hair, since the razor terrified her — hung in ragged tangles.

"His death is a natural thing," Jarha was saying. "Wahankh's life was a long one, and it was time for him to leave us."

Jarha looked perfect, as always. Kohl shadowed his eyes in precise symmetry, untouched by tears. His black wig shone in the light. When he moved, the light danced across clinking gold jewelry.

Wahankh's jewelry, Peshet thought bitterly. Already Jarha took Wahankh's place as master of this home.

He placed a manicured hand on Ruia's shoulder and squeezed gently. "I share your pain."

"I miss Peshet, too." Ruia bit her lip and turned away.

"Your father would have wanted Peshet with him. He deserved the company of his loyal scribe. Peshet was right when she chose to stay with him." He moved closer and wrapped his arms around her.

When I chose to stay? Peshet wanted to scream. *Can't you see what he's doing?* But of course, Ruia couldn't. Though older than Peshet, the girl had the mentality of a small child. An accident when she was younger had cracked her skull and injured her brain. She lacked the cynicism to see through this snake as he tightened his coils around her.

But Peshet could see. *You can kill me,* she said soundlessly. *You will not have her.*

In this form, freed from the flesh, it was easier to draw upon the power of her *ka.* She traced the hieroglyph for death, drawing the sarcophagus again and again over Jarha's chest. The power grew within her, fighting for release. She would reach into him and squeeze his heart until it burst, destroying him from the inside.

He would make Ruia his wife, then his slave. He would flaunt his infidelities and twist her mind until she blamed herself for his dalliances. He might even kill her once he had no further need for her.

The pressure grew, fighting to be free. Her vision

sparked as she tried to control it. She had never attempted this sort of magic. It writhed and lashed like an asp struggling for release. She tried to focus it on Jarha, but her grasp was too weak. Her hand began to shake, disrupting the hieroglyphs.

"No," she cried. She tried to regain control. Like the asp, the power twisted in her grip and turned on her. Death poured through her *ka*, and she screamed in silence as the house disappeared into darkness.

SHE AND RUIA had stood together, watching as Wahankh's embalmed body was placed into the first of several wooden boxes that would go into the ornate stone sarcophagus.

"He took me into his home," Peshet whispered. "He gave me a family."

Ruia offered her a cup of dark wine. "To make you feel better."

"Thank you," Peshet said. Normally, she avoided the foreign drink, but today the bitter taste was a welcome thing.

The girl smiled. "Jarha told me it would help you," she said with satisfaction. "He said to drink as much as you like, and that it would make your troubles pass more swiftly."

Peshet was still staring in horror at the cup in her hands when Jarha walked into the room. He handed her a black, double-handled clay jug. "The wine was imported from Knossos at great cost, for your palate alone," he said. "I suggest you take it with you, to hasten your journey."

It was too late to do anything. Peshet knew, even without seeing the smug gleam in his eyes, that the wine was poisoned. It was a perfect trap. She was already dead, and if she told Ruia what he had done, it would destroy her too. She would blame herself for giving Peshet the poisoned drink. Knowing Ruia, the guilt could drive her to take her own life.

Peshet had been helpless as the seizures ripped Wahankh's life from his body. She would not be responsible for Ruia's death as well.

"Come, Ruia," Jarha said. "Let us leave the scribe to her thoughts."

They walked out of the room, leaving Peshet alone with the embalmers. She placed a hand on the smooth, bleached wood and whispered, "At least I will be with you soon."

SOMETHING scraped her face. She opened her eyes and stared into Bast-ta-sherit's long, narrow face. The cat licked her left eyelid, apparently enjoying the grease in the kohl.

She started to sit up, and a thousand blacksmiths hammered her skull. She groaned. The cat leapt away, fur bristling. She tried to speak, but her throat was dry as the sand.

The muscles of her right hand were cramped. She managed to bring it to her face without too much pain, and found herself looking into the eye of Sitma-at, the badge she had left to anchor herself to this place. The badge had left its imprint in the lines of her palm. A shudder tore through her as she realized how close she had come to losing her *ka* forever.

The cat reached out to paw the gold badge.

Without warning, her body spasmed as the poison sent blades of pain through her gut and chest. The cat hissed and jumped back again, watching warily until her muscles unlocked and she managed to breathe again.

"I'm sorry to startle you."

Bast-ta-sherit's tail lashed furiously, and he continued to glare.

"I failed him," she whispered. "He brought me into his home, treated me like a second daughter, and I failed him."

The cat walked over to rub his head against her knee. Somehow, his presence dulled the edge of her grief and fear. If she was to die, she would not die alone.

The pain of her spell gradually faded, though the burning of the poison remained. Peshet forced herself to sit upright. Her shoulders scraped the limestone wall. Bast-ta-sherit nudged her hand.

"I'm dying, and you want your ears scratched," she grumbled. The cat shoved her again, unrepenting.

She began to stroke the wiry fur behind his ears. "For so long, I was jealous of Ruia. *I* wanted to be the daughter of Wahankh. I was so much smarter than her, yet fate put me second for his affections.

"He made me work hours at a time, copying old scrolls and books while Ruia ran and played like a child half her age. It disgusted me. Once, I even went so far as to hit her."

Wahankh had come running the instant he heard Ruia's cries. "What happened?" he demanded in a voice that set Peshet's insides quivering.

Ruia stared at them both with wide, confused eyes. "Nothing, father." A moment later, she fled to her room, leaving Peshet to face him alone.

"Go with her," he said gruffly. "I have no time for this."

Walking into Ruia's room was a harsher punishment than anything else Wahankh could have done. The girl sat with her knees clutched to her chest. She said nothing as Peshet stormed in, furious at the world and at herself.

"Well? Are you hurt?"

Ruia shook her head. "I didn't mean to get you in trouble," she said softly.

Peshet blinked in disbelief. "It's not your fault," she heard herself say. For the first time, she saw the admiration, the love shining up from Ruia's eyes.

As she continued to pet the cat, she whispered, "Can you understand what it was like, Bast-ta-sherit? All that time, she had looked up to me like an older sister. Like *family*. I started to cry. It took more than an hour to convince her my tears weren't her fault.

"The next day, I confessed to Wahankh. I told him my actions were unforgivable, and I would accept whatever punishment he thought fitting.

"Wahankh smiled. 'Responsibility is the keystone of wisdom,' he said. He said he was proud of the way I had made up to Ruia.

"That was the day he began to teach me magic."

THE FAINT LIGHT from the *ka* tunnels had turned blood red as Ra's light vanished for the night, and the oil in the lamp was almost gone. Soon the tomb would plunge into blackness. Once that happened, Peshet would never see the light again.

She was growing weaker. Her hands trembled constantly now, and her muscles felt like water.

"You must look after her," she told the cat, hoping Bast would hear.

Bast-ta-sherit chewed at his paw, ignoring her.

"I failed. I couldn't protect her."

The cat still refused to look at her.

"Jarha had only been with us for a few months," she said. "He was the son of a nobleman, and claimed kinship with the Priest of Yinepu, so Wahankh could not turn him away. Jarha's sister would be the one to inherit his family's wealth, so he was searching for a way to build his own fortune. Wahankh was well-off and widely respected. More importantly, he had a daughter who could be easily wooed."

The memories refocused her anger. Jarha had lurked about town, plying the gossips with money and drink until he learned of Wahankh's sickness. His sickness, and the pliability of his daughter.

Bast-ta-sherit glared with a sternness that matched Wahankh's as Peshet crawled back to the circle. "I have to try again."

The cat walked up to her, and tiny sickle-claws sliced her forearm before she could begin.

She jerked back as parallel lines of blood began to flow. "What else can I do?" she pleaded. Deep down, she knew the cat was correct. If she tried this, it would destroy her. But what choice did she have? She would rather have her *ka* scattered to the desert than face Wahankh after failing to protect his daughter.

Bast-ta-sherit raised his chin and waited, unblinking, like a disappointed father.

She had to destroy Jarha. The man was a crocodile who preyed on human flesh. Ruia would never be able to protect herself from him.

The cat mewed softly.

Slowly, her muddled mind began to understand. Ruia was unable to protect herself from *anyone*. Destroying Jarha would only leave her alone, and there was nothing she feared more. It would kill her as effectively as Jarha's poisoned wine.

"What do you want me to do?"

The lamp-light reflected greenly from the cat's eyes as he gazed patiently at her. Wahankh had once told her that cats captured the sun's light in their eyes, and that was how they could see through the darkness. They were creatures of Bast, bringing light and darkness together in those keen eyes.

"Light and darkness," Peshet whispered. And suddenly she knew what she must do.

"QUICKLY, before the lamp dies."

The spell of binding was to be performed at midday, under the gaze of Ra. With the sun already set, it might not work. But if Bast-ta-sherit truly carried the light of the sun in his eyes. . . .

Finding one of Ruia's belongings was easy. The girl had placed several small, decorated vases in the tomb to accompany her father. Peshet selected one with a gold rim and an image of Isis glazed into the side. She set this in the center of the new circle. Broken bits of wax were all that remained of her earlier spell. This would be a far simpler magic, a single hieroglyph imbued with the power of her *ka*.

But first, she needed something of Jarha's. He had placed gifts into the tomb, of course. Jarha never failed to observe proper etiquette. But his gifts had come from Wahankh's own household. She recognized everything he had placed in the corner of the tomb.

She refused to believe that his selfishness would save him. The world could not be so cruel. But without something of his, the spell would fail. A trinket, a piece of jewelry, anything.

The cat meowed softly. Peshet glanced up, following his gaze. And for the first time in days, she laughed.

The jug of poisoned wine joined Ruia's vase in the center of the circle. When she was ready, Bast-ta-sherit took his place at the head of the circle and waited, eyes wide.

Sunfire gleamed in the cat's eyes, almost as bright as the dying oil lamp as she began the spell. The candles had long since burned out, but she arranged the scraps of wax around the jug and the vase. Two vertical lines, and the hieroglyph of a twined rope. Her hands shook as she spread the wax, nudging the white specks into place.

She touched the vase with one finger and caught the impression of innocence, tinged with pain. "Ruia," she whispered, smiling as she touched her sister. She stretched out her other hand.

Touching the jug was like grabbing white-hot coals. Anger and desperation seared through her. There was also something else, something hidden. Eventually, she identified fear.

Jarha was afraid of her. That was why he had been so desperate to be rid of her. He feared she would force him from Wahankh's home, leaving him poor and alone.

"You have no more cause for fear," Peshet whispered as she began the spell, whispering a prayer to Hathor, the Netjert of love. The spell was little more than the blessing spoken at every marriage celebration. The words came easily to Peshet's dry lips.

Jarha would soon persuade Ruia to marry him. But after this spell, they would be joined under Hathor, a joining witnessed by Ra himself. Any harm done to one would be shared by the other. Ruia's pain, physical or emotional, would be Jarha's own. His self-centered nature would lead him to protect Ruia at every turn, simply to insure his own safety.

Peshet smiled. She would set one crocodile to guard Ruia from the rest. It was even possible that, some day, he might truly come to care for her.

But as the power grew, all Peshet knew was that she would soon be able to rejoin her mentor.

HOURS LATER, a sleek tomcat emerged from the top of a recently constructed tomb. He stretched, bathing in the silver moonlight and the cool night air. Then he leapt gracefully onto the grassy sands below and vanished into the darkness.   ❖

Jim C. Hines' second fantasy novel, Goblin Hero, *was released in May of 2007. The third goblin book will be out . . . well, that depends on when he finishes revisions. He lives in Michigan with his wife and two children. They share their home with 2.75 cats, one of which has recently begun losing his fur. Jim sympathizes.*

CREEPER SHADOWS

by Fred Chappell

H AUGHTY, HARD-EYED, horse-faced: I formed no favorable impression of this tall woman in her long gray smock whom the slender young footman had summoned forth. I was not tuneful in temper anyway; and when she inquired my name and business, I handed her Astolfo's letter of introduction without giving response except for a grudging nod. She swept away brusquely, leaving me alone in the foyer.

She had understood me to be a servant like herself, but I took pride to stand as confidential aide to Astolfo, the acknowledged master of shadows of the port city of Tardocco, of the long coastal province of Tlemia, and of all the known world beside.

I had dressed with particular care in forest-green doublet above tawny trunks, shining black calf-length boots spotless of mud, even though I had walked from Astolfo's mid-town villa across Tardocco to this manse of Esquire Sativius on the outskirts. Red gloves with silver piping, I had donned; and my wine-red cap sported a brash white plume. It should be obvious that I was no low menial, yet that equinous woman had taken but cursory notice of my finery.

Nor did she hasten to return, and so I took leisurely stock of my surroundings. The house was a rambling two-story edifice of weathered gray brick. A bay window checkered with glass and alabaster panes fronted the protruding second story that overhung the portico with its sturdy oaken columns. The foyer floor was of unpolished flagstone; and the door that led to the farther rooms, now closed to me, was of lightly varnished chestnut. In short, here was just the sort of domicile one would expect to enter when visiting the wealthy merchant rope-dealer Matteo Sativius.

I drew four deep breaths, nerve-wary because this was the first commission of any true import that Astolfo had entrusted to my care *solus*. Five swift and crowded seasons I had spent in his employ, after first insulting his dignity by breaking into his house, allowing myself to be apprehended, and then throwing myself upon his mercies with entreaties almost tearful to be taken into his services. It was my ambition then and after to make of myself what I conjectured him to be, the cleverest and most successful thief who ever filched a shadow from a heedless caster. Five seasons of grueling training under the large and horny hand of his dumb manservant Mutano, five years of scanning weevilish books and manuals, of grubby little tasks and assignments, of unending but cheerful contumely and admonition: This harsh period had steeled my disposition, I fancied. It was a course of life much like preparing for a priesthood, except that at the end of it, I hoped to amass wealth in golden hillocks innumerable instead of some airy bower in a painted paradise.

Astolfo had told me little of this present affair in hand. " 'Tis some difficulty concerning the umbrae of children," he said. "I am otherwise occupied just now, and so I leave all to you. There may be a plumpish fee. This Sativius is reputed generous."

"Will Mutano accompany me?" I asked, thinking that if there were danger involved I should be glad of the presence of my overlarge and humorously bellicose drill-master.

"Mutano has in train a serious personal business,"

Astolfo said. "He may require your assistance as it progresses. He is already enlisting the aid of Creeper."

"Of Creeper?" I was not easily surprised these days by what I learned of and from Astolfo, but now I was astonished. Creeper is the largest and blackest of all the sixteen cats that haunt the grounds and outbuildings of the villa. Mutano had never evinced fondness for Creeper or for any other of the feline troop.

The shadow master shrugged his rounded shoulders, spread his nimble, maidenly-seeming hands in a dismissive gesture, and said, "They are spheres unto themselves, the man and the cat. I know only that Mutano is engaged with the animal for endless hours and I know the nature of the task he has set himself and he holds it to be of the greatest importance."

"And he wishes me to aid him?"

"So he has signaled."

That was another imponderable conceit, that my master in the arts of the sword and of the shadow-sundering blades, of purse-snipping, lock-tickling, and so forth, might desire, even perhaps require, my assistance. He had always fixed me in a most sardonic regard.

The train of my suppositions broke sharply when the gangly, gray-smocked woman returned and with the crooking of a finger bade me follow her through a large salon muffled with carpet and darkened with wall hangings, up the stair and around a gallery into the room of the bay window.

She ushered me into the presence of Esquire Sativius and his spouse Funisia and retreated toward the doorway, making me feel rather as if I had been deposited before the older couple as a lump of merchandise, a chair or washstand, to be considered for purchase.

It did not suit that the light from the bay window flooded their figures from behind, making their faces dark, so I began to sidle little by little, making a leg here and a bow there, in a half circle until the light was more in my favor.

Making much show of it, Sativius broke Astolfo's seal, unfolded the heavy page, and took his own good while perusing what would have been only a short letter. When he had done, he gazed upon me with a frown that almost knit his bushy white eyebrows together.

I judged him to be of sound middle age, with his silvered beard jutting over his wimpled collar and his smooth hands emerging from starchy, frilled cuffs. He wore a short sword of ceremonial utility only.

"I had expected your master to come to my summons," he said. His voice was soft but held reserves of authority.

"Maestro Astolfo tenders his regrets," I replied. "A mortally urgent business close touching upon his person prevents his presence. I am his confidential secretary Falco, as I think his letter informs you. I am authorized to act on his behalf in every particular."

He turned to look at his wife Funisia. She was some deal younger than her man, with a face that retained much of its youth, a comely countenance. In figure she was not tall but there was a grace about her that suggested tallness. Her dress was modest, with full skirt, dark-blue silk bodice open only at the clavicles, her dark hair worn in a braid coiled around the crown. Her only jewel was a small diamond set in a wedding ring. Demurely she met her husband's gaze with a smile and a brief nod.

"You will make report to Maestro Astolfo replete with all detail?"

"Assuredly."

"In brief, then, the case is this: Funisia and I are the parents of twins, the one a boy and older by less than an hour, t'other a girl. Except for the difference of the sexes, they are identical. They are devoted each to the other and are reluctant to part company for any reasons, even for those of those of necessity of nature. They never argue or quarrel; even their sharpest disagreements are sweetly couched. We have doted upon them perhaps too closely, they being the offspring of our early middle years. Yet, tightly as we kept watch, we failed to note a fault in their two physiques and were astonished to find it out. It came to our notice only this sennight past."

"Is it not a defect a medico might reflect upon?" I asked.

"Only one of our children possesses a shadow," Sativius said. "The other is quite bare of any umbra whatsoever."

I stood silent for a moment, trying to fix the conceit in my mind. "One shadow only between them?"

"Yes."

"To which of them belongeth the shadow, lad or lass?"

"We cannot say. When they are close together it seems to attach to the both of them at once. When they are separate, it will go to one or other as it seems to choose."

"And you first took stock of this debility only these fourteen days ago?"

" 'Twas but twelve days," he said. "Funisia first took note when she was reading to them from a book of fables."

"They were standing before me as I sat in a chair by the table there," she said, indicating with a nod the table behind me that was placed before the bay window. "They remained stock still, as always they do, to attend the tale of the jolly cobbler and the shoeless witch. The candles stood on the table by my right hand; and when I looked up from the page, I saw what I saw."

"May the children be brought forth?" I asked and when they dispatched Mistress High Horse to fetch them, I requested that candles be set along the table. There was good light through the window, but more would be useful.

The candles were arranged and lit, and Graysmock led in the children. They came forward to stand before me with Sativius on one side and their mother on the other. I gazed upon them curiously, for they made a striking pair.

They were pale of complexion, almost nacreous, like

the pearly oyster shell. Slim in figure with blond hair verging on silvery, they were clad in black knee breeches and black jackets and stockinged in shining white silk. Large silver buckles were set upon their black, square-toed shoes. The boy's hair was longer than the girl's and only this single distinction marked them apart, for otherwise they were as identical in appearance as any two raindrops. They looked up at me fearlessly, their bright gray eyes seeming as large as glass doorknobs in their delicate faces. They were wraithlike, and I discerned with my first perusal that they would be taciturn younglings; expectant silence hung about them like that preceding the onset of a nocturnal snowfall.

I smiled and said my name and they did not reply.

Their silence was perhaps of no great concern, for I was employed to look about their shadows, or the lack thereof, yet I tried to take stock of all that I could, for I knew that Maestro Astolfo would query me closely.

They stood before me, a hand-span apart, and behind them lay a single shadow of ordinary appearance, except that it seemed darker in tone than I might have expected. Considering that this darkening might be an effect of the darkish carpet on which they stood, I requested their parents to part them, widening the space between by another hand-span. The shadow did not alter its shape, though it should have begun to split apart where it joined the feet of the children. Farther and farther apart we posed them until an arm's length separated the pair and still the shadow did not split, though it became difficult to discern where its nether attachment was located. At last, Sativius and Funisia placed their children a long lance-length apart and the shadow, without a motion visible to my observation, no longer attached to the girl but only to the boy. Behind her, light held all the floor-place where shade should lie.

"You seem to have lost one of your valuables, little mistress," I said. I gave her the most gently ingratiating smile I could muster. "What is your name?"

She gazed at me with those great luminous eyes and remained as silent as a melting snowflake.

"She is called Rudensia," her mother said. "Her brother is Rudens."

I bowed to the children. "I am honored to make the acquaintance of so unusual a brace of youth," I said, though the phrases sounded clumsy. In fact, all my efforts at playful diplomacy fell out lame and gauche, and I discarded the notion of trying to become friendly with the strange children.

We repeated the experiment three times again, with the result that Rudensia lost her shadow once to her brother while he twice lost his to her. I was unable to see how the transference occurred, yet the motion of it — if there had been a motion — was neither swift nor gradual. At one time it was simply there, stretched out behind the lad, and next time it fell behind the girl.

"What is to be done?" Funisia asked softly. Her eyes were fearful.

"I must study upon the phenomenon," I said, "but I have every confidence that all shall be resolved in happy manner."

"I do wish Maestro Astolfo had seen fit to answer my call," Sativius said. "I begin to harbor hard feeling upon that head."

"I shall make full report to him concerning every aspect," I replied. "It may be that he can post-pone some part of his business and make a visitation."

These words did not mollify the rope merchant, but I had not expected that they would effect any change in his temper. Still, I could not allow such awkwardness to put me out of countenance; this, my first task to be delegated to my own stratagems I held too important to be disfigured by trifles.

I took my leave, promising to return soon with the best and most fully detailed prognosis I could mount; and, though both parents received my pledge with dull grace, I felt my visit must conclude. Making my manners, I edged toward the door. Graysmock opened it and escorted me down the stair, through the foyer, and out into the cool midday where a threat of rain was steadily increasing. I hastened my stride, hoping to arrive under Astolfo's roof before the clouds let go.

I LOOKED FOR Astolfo first in the kitchen where he was often to be found, perched on the great butcher's block in the center of the room, dangling his legs, thumping his heels on the wood as he spun out the filament of his long, intricate thoughts. He was not there, nor was he in the larger library with the tall lancet windows and the hanging brass lamps. He was not in the small library either; but in this cozier room, with its book-strewn table and leathern armchairs and friendly small hearth, I chanced upon Mutano.

He gave me a noncommittal salute and returned to his disport with Creeper, pursuing a game that any babbling child might play with a cat, teasingly jigging a scrap of paper tied to a thread and whisking it away when the animal pounced. An idle pastime, methought. Where was the grave business with Creeper of which Astolfo had spoken? I settled into an armchair to await the shadow master's arrival. Rain had begun to lash the ivied walls of the villa and nothing else seemed so pleasurable as to sit at ease for a spell, finding pictures in the flames and hearkening to the fray of the elements.

The fire comported itself in no ordinary fashion. It brightened and dimmed and sent a roiling, misty smoke out over the hearth, a vapor that retained a defined shape and was not of the arbitrary formlessness of familiar hearth-fire smoke.

Against the gently leaping flames, the smoke-shape was difficult to define precisely, but the longer I observed, the more knowable it became. Then I realized that its writhings and saltations, its turnings and moilings, were like those of a cat at play. The mist-form creature was aping, as 'twere an image in a mirror, the motions of Creeper as he cavorted, twisted, and feinted the air in merry chase of Mutano's dancing scrap of paper.

I rose and drew closer, trying to discover of what substance this active shape consisted; it was so airy and light and agile that it must have been composed of the most æthereal of stuffs. Soon I knew it to be a shadow, the true shadow of Creeper, even though it was not attached to the green-eyed cat at any point of the body.

Here I beheld a marvel I had only heard rumored. When a shadow is taken from its subject, be that caster ever so active, ever so fluent with sinew and *vis vitae*, the shade, as a rule, loses all inner spirit and lies or stands or hangs inert. It retains its volumes and textures, its tints and tones, and something of its flavors and aromas. Astolfo is capable of detecting, so saith he, certain sounds belonging to a severed shadow, small noises like distant echoes from a lost valley. He is the master. And animation requires a skill and, beyond that, an amplitude of art that I was certain Mutano did not possess, so Astolfo must have had some hand in this accomplishment.

While I sat down again and pleasured in the music of rain-sweep against our walls, Astolfo came sprightly into the room, paused briefly to smile at the antics of Mutano and Creeper, and beckoned me to follow him to the kitchen where he poured for the both of us a dollop of sweet, resinous wine into thick glass beakers.

Thus he commenced: "How went the intercourse with the rope merchant? Have you learned to escape the wiles of the rope-maker's daughter?"

I was mystified; the pale Rudensia was but a child. Then I understood that he used thieves' language; "the rope-maker's daughter" is an alehouse term for the hangman's noose. "I learn some new thing every day," I replied.

"Tell me then of your dealings with Esquire Sativius."

In slow and careful words, I gave him as minute an account of the encounter as I was able, trying to omit naught that might be worthy of notice. Seated on the butcher's block with his head inclined toward me, he almost seemed to twitch his large ears as I spoke.

When I concluded, he sat silent for long moments. "How many years of age hang on these children?"

"Thirteen."

His expression grew grave. "This matter may be of a darker character than we have suspicioned. Would you describe their shared shadow to me again? Come as close to the object as may be."

When I repeated my impressions with some slight enlargement, he still seemed unsatisfied.

"You say this shadow that lay between them was darker of tint that you would otherwise observe in the circumstance?"

"So it appeared there."

"Was it uniform of its darkness or was the center of it perhaps a little more dark than its flanks?"

"It lay upon a wine-colored carpet of thickish pile," I said. "I could distinguish no gradation."

"Close your eyes. Envision all again."

I did so, but with no result. I shook my head.

"The mother and the father spoke, but the children spoke not?"

"Yes."

"Suppose that they had spoken. Which voice would be louder, that of the boy or of the girl?"

I considered. "They would be equally soft," I said, "with something of the timbre as of the pealing of little silver bells. But they did not speak."

"How did you form your conjecture as to the sound of their voices?"

"I do not know. Yet the soft bell-peal comparison cometh vivid to mind."

He nodded. "Now close your eyes and envision the shadow where it lay on the carpet. Only do not think about it."

I closed my eyes, deepened my breathing, and relaxed the concentration of my mind. Then I saw what I had seen. "The center of the shadow is indeed darker than the larger body of it. Yet that center bears the same outline as the greater shadow. It is like an inner shadow of the greater shadow."

"Doth this dark one rest content where it lies?"

I did not hesitate. "It is a shadow," I said. "The ways

of its thought — if it possess any of that — I never could say in an æon of attempt."

"Could you declare if the parents are affectionate of their progeny?"

"I believe them so."

"Might one of them be more so than the other?"

"That is possible," I said. "When they turned them about-face to depart the room, the mother Funisia rested her hand for a moment on her daughter's shoulder. Sativius did not bestow that small gesture upon his son."

He hesitated long before he spoke again. "This piece of business I have given over to your care, and it belongs to you to conclude successfully. But I will tell you somewhat of similar circumstances that I have heard in my years. I do so to be of some aid, yet not to direct the affair myself. It is in your charge. I desire also to impress upon you the gravity of this state of things.

"These children now approach that time when 'swift-wing'd desire,' as the poets name it, first makes its trembling advance within mind and body. Those who have been innocently affectionate as childhood playmates commence to look upon each other with new eyes. They may join in amorous union. This act brothers and sisters ordinarily will not perform, but they may draw together more tightly in mind and spirit than ever before and at last become almost a single entity. These pale-souled children of Sativius already share but one shadow. Soon they may possess only the one soul between them. If this annealment takes place and then at a later season they are parted by some turning of fate, one of them will surely die. Both may well perish."

"What would be the case if they were separated now, before the tumult of early desire comes upon them?"

"With only one shadow between them, one or t'other would pine away to sickness and live out a life of pallid misery."

"I can foresee no happy result for the dilemma," I said.

"Have you no glimmering of a notion? I thought when I found you in the library that you might be setting out upon a course of research."

"I had thought I might pursue the genealogical line," I said. "Perhaps this strange malady has been recorded of the Sativius family in time past. If such a case has been historied, perhaps a remedy may have been noted down. I have also conjectured that an ancestral curse might have been laid upon the family by a rival family or by an unknown foe."

"Beware that you do not mire in superstitious notions concerning inimical spells of witch and warlock. Keep to the science of sciomancy. There may be something in the genealogical tables; you know where the records are shelved. But I will also suggest that you thumb some way through the pages of Morosius."

"Morosius? *Annales tenebrae antiquitatae?*"

This was a tome I held in especial disfavor, a dull, bulky volume of confused accounts from every era and territory of miraculous or preternatural phenomena: fairies that infested bakeries, toads with jewels in their foreheads, flying anvils, drowned monasteries, and so forth. Morosius was particularly fond of peculiar rains falling out of clear blue skies — pebbles, emeralds, thimbles, goats, hay carts, thunderstones, powdered wigs, &c. All this farrago of hearsay and cloudy testimonia was flung upon the pages artlessly, so that one had no indication where to find relatable information.

"I seem to recall there was some story of a statue and its shadow," Astolfo said. "But it has been long since I perused the book."

"I shall look into it," I said. My promise was half-hearted.

"Let us hope these children are not victims of some angry plot," Astolfo said.

"We shall have enough dealings with a vengeful opponent when Mutano brings his quest for justice into full career."

"What is happening with Mutano?"

" 'Twill be a sober amusement," Astolfo said. "You shall know all of it that is needful sooner than you may desire. . . . But do not let me keep you from the library and the family trees and the learned but mazy sentences of Morosius."

Mutano had departed the library, but the hearthfire needed only a little encouragement with a poker and a taste of unseasoned oak to set it crackling merrily. I fetched the requisite volumes of genealogical history to the armchair by the fireside, piled them in a stack of five, seized the topmost, and set to tracing the mainstream and tributaries of the race of Sativius. Soon enough I discerned that there would be little of interest in these histories. 'Twas but the old story of a race of yeomen farmers descended from soldiery. There once had been a great estate, but it had divided into smaller and smaller parcels as inheritors multiplied. The offspring of the former landowners joined the mercenary armies that formerly ranged the countryside or they went to sea or entered into various trades in the newly burgeoning towns.

The man Paolo Sativius, father of the twins, had first followed the sea where he studied the gear and tackle and trim of ships, borrowed money from his father when he abandoned the sail, and founded a rope-making enterprise which incorporated certain improvements in hempen-ware he had devised as a tar.

Of the mother's lineage, little was recorded. I traced a few branches of farmers, petty tradesmen, and undistinguished warriors and let the book drop from my hand.

The rain had increased its force; the windows creaked as the storm beat upon the panes; drops sizzled as they fell down the chimney into the flames. The pleasure of the hour was so calm and somnolent I did not desire to distress it by reading in musty old Morosius, but duty impelled me to return the genealogical tables to their appointed shelves and drag down the heavy folio of the *Annales* and lug it back to my seat. I predicted that it would work its soporific powers so efficaciously that these leaden paragraphs would put me slumbering.

But it is the way of certain books to present a different character to us each time we open them. The rain, the tall stillness of the room, the hearth-fire with the clump of massy shadow there in the ingle: These surroundings caused Moroisus to seem an appropriate companion.

I searched first for any story about a statue since Astolfo would surely rogate me upon the point. But all I discovered was a tale concerning a certain well-loved priest, Prester Vonnard, who enjoyed in his lifetime such high esteem among the populace of his little village of Zenoro that they decided to erect a statue to him and perform an unveiling ceremony lavish with encomious speeches and the solemn chant of a children's chorus.

But when the canvas was swept away from the bronze figure of this paragon of virtue it was seen by one and all that the shadow the statue cast upon the paving stones was of a vivid scarlet hue and seemed in texture almost as viscid as blood. A prudent but close investigation of the life of Vonnard was ordered, and in a short time the statue was removed and the bronze melted and fashioned into armor. The shadow remained, however, an immutable stain; and any traveler to Zenoro still may inspect it. Morosius is, however, silent about the location of Zenoro.

Turning a few idle pages, I chanced upon a speculation by an unnamed philosopher who conjectured that if a lion eat a man, the shadow of the lion will contain, as an envelope contains a document, the shadow of that misfortunate and that this shadow, though indistinguishable, will not be part of the lion's shadow but a separate thing. The man is a spirit superior to the lion, saith this sage, and therefore can never be truly assimilated by an inferior spirit. 'Twas an interesting thought, but I reflected it must provide but small comfort to the man.

One overladen chapter was devoted to the Specter of the Summit, a phenomenon of northern latitudes that I had heard Astolfo discourse upon. A walker approaching the peak of a mountain cloaked in cold mist, and with the obscured sun behind him, will see a shadow advancing toward him and growing larger in its progress. Then, if the mist lighten but a little, he will see his own shadow, darker in hue, cast upon — within — the approaching shadow. At a certain point, depending upon the light and the density of the mist, both shadows disappear. Some overcurious travelers have tumbled into gorges trying to gain closer inspection of this phenomenon.

These were the passages that teased my attention. Other pages excoriating Morosius's rival philosophers or speculating whether the shadow of a rose truly possesses an odor or only the memory of one, &c., &c., I passed over with scant interest. But these instances of shadows-within-shadows seemed to point in a favorable direction, and as I reflected upon them I fell into a contented doze.

My sleep was shortened by a difficulty in breathing. There was some obstruction to inhalation, at first so subtle I thought it part of a dream. It grew thicker about my mouth and nose and when I opened my eyes the room with its windows and candles was darkened as by a pall of smoke. I raised my hands to my face to claw away this weave of fog when it went from me suddenly. It gathered into a ball and then elongated to a ferret-like shape and streaked grayly over the worn carpet to the door. Now, of course, I recognized it as the shadow of Creeper.

Mutano was in another room, directing the movement of the large cat. He had found some way to position the animal so that its palpable shadow here in the library had covered my face and hindered my breath. Mutano was fond of vexing me with jests of corporeal nature and after so many of them I had grown impatient. I called down curses on his square-jawed, shaggy head.

That is, I attempted to mutter these imprecations, but found that no sounds came from me. I tried again and then again, but all I could manage to utter was a raspy whisper that lacked any trace of my normal timbre. A brass ewer of water stood on a near table and I poured a beaker full and drank it down in three swallows, but there was no aid in it. My voice had departed my voice-box.

Everyone is familiar with the superstition that cats can steal away the breath of sleeping children and cause them to perish by suffocation. That is an old wives' tale, foolish in every respect. Yet now the shadow of a cat had reived away my voice. So I supposed the case to be, at any rate, and went in angry search of Mutano.

I HAD NOT FAR to look. The kitchen was occupied by Mutano and Astolfo, and Creeper. Astolfo had taken his place, seated on the butcher block, while Mutano stood by a long counter beneath the west window. Creeper was crouched on the window ledge; and I observed when, at a sign from Mutano, the big cat leapt down from the ledge and covered a boule of wheaten bread on the counter with his body. I knew that in whatever other room his shadow was, it too was leaping down upon an object and embracing it closely.

Mutano gave a wide and happy and infuriating grin when he saw me watching, and my impulse was to return his japery with an arse-kick, but Astolfo held up his hand to restrain me.

"This is no inane trickery, Falco," he said. "It is instead a demonstration of part of a plan Mutano has formed to get his voice back from one who has made himself his mortal enemy."

I tried to speak but only buzzed like a cicada.

"Sit you by the oven," Astolfo directed. "Quaff a glass of ale. The tale is soon told and you must hear it before you accompany Mutano upon his mission of restoration."

I did as told. The light, nutty ale soothed my throat and calmed a little my disposition.

"It is the old story of rivalry for a woman's favors," Astolfo said. "This was the lady Stellina, a bright, beautiful woman of petite figure and immense charm. Have you not noticed how these broad-beamed bravos, thick-necked and huge-handed, are so often attracted by small females doll-like and delicate of feature?"

I watched Mutano stroke Creeper and saw in my mind's eye how the cat's shadow, wherever it was, would be writhing with delight. Astolfo's description of his manservant was a just one: broad-beamed, thick-necked, huge-handed. He might have added knuckle-scarred; excessively muscular; and, as a drill-master, too joyfully severe.

"Stellina, the daughter of the Count Rolando of the Lovoso Marches, had harbored a taste for the large and horny-palmed lads since she was a child. Now that she had come into her eighteenth year, she was able to inform her taste with a wide experience and, after trying the pleasures of a strong dozen specimens of manhood, settled upon Mutano as one of her favorites.

"The other was a tall, lean, hawk-featured young felon named Castilio from one of the western isles. He was a stranger to the garrison town of Rupz where Count Orlando maintained a private militia. Quick-tempered and sharp-tongued, he was ready to battle man or beast as facile whimsy dictated. Such reckless-ness appealed to Stellina's mineral heart. She had not heard about his abducting of maidens of too-tender years and despoiling them with brutal handling. Or if she had heard, she cared naught.

"Yet she also liked Mutano who, though less quick-witted than Castilio and less blade-eager, showed an easy good humor of sardonic cast. He feared nothing. In particular, he showed no fear of Castilio and only deigned to acknowledge his rival's existence when Stellina bestowed on the lean fellow some mischie-vous epithet of high praise. In those days, Mutano was known for the quality of his voice — resonant, mellif-luous, and compelling. He might have made his way in life as a minstrel had not the martial exertions claimed his allegiance.

"I will abbreviate this long romance of the foolish young. The rivalry developed to such a fevered heat

that Castilio, in a fit of jealous imbecility, challenged
Mutano to a wrestling match. Almost any other kind
of combat might have favored the challenger, for Mutano has an especial liking for stuffing the elbows of
his opponents into their ears and twisting their spines
into sheep's-head knots. The contest concluded in the
space of time it takes to sing one of Zandrio's ballads."

I sipped at the ale and tried my voice once more. It
was beginning to return a little, I thought.

"Castilio was as vengeful as he was foul-tempered
and he vowed to take from Mutano one of his proudest
possessions, his beautiful voice. So he invited our
friend to a drinking session at a villainous inn whose
proprietor was his crony. This occasion was supposed
to mark a truce between them, and I believe Mutano
expected his rival to renounce upon this hour all claim
to Stellina, the golden object of their double desires.

"Mutano mounted the steps to a small room, as had
been arranged. The room stood in dim light when he
arrived, but when he fed more wick to the lamp on the
table, he wished that it had been submerged in blackness. There, bound to a chair across the room, was the
naked body of Stellina. Her throat had been torn out.
Her features were contorted in agony; and her body
bore dread, gaping wounds."

"Horrible!" My voice sounded, a croaking whisper.

"Yes. You can imagine the great shriek that Mutano uttered. All his strength was behind the force of
his voice and in that moment it was taken from him,
captured. Castilio was in the room with a trio of cruel
rogues, and he had with him a device that enabled
him to steal the sound of Mutano's melodious voice.
He took it from him and holds it captive still. Now
Mutano determines to repossess his voice. What other
designs he has upon the fate of Castilio, I do not
know."

"But —"

"Oh yes," Astolfo said. He smiled and shook his
head. "That was no corpse of Stellina bound in a chair
but only a waxwork effigy of the woman, disfigured

and maimed. The only purpose of this waxen mammet was to extract a great shriek of grief and outrage from Mutano so that it might be captured."

"How can one make captive a voice?" I asked, pleased that my own was at last returning. I drank the ale cup dry and poured a smidgin more.

"With an ingenious series of wooden boxes, nested inside one another, with sufficient space between their neighbor walls that the echo of a voice rebounds within, again and again, until in the final, smallest box it is reduced to the essence of itself. You understand that I must speak in metaphors. Truly to describe this complicated device would require a long string of geometrical demonstrations, as well as some discourse upon the theorem of sound as being transferred from one place to another by a succession of æthereal waves. For our present purposes, it is enough to know that Castilio holds Mutano's power of speech in thrall and that our colleague has laid a scheme to gain it back."

"But how may a voice be preserved over a period of time? It consists of breath and must soon fade back into its airy elemental state. No wonder-box, ingenious as it may be, is capable of preserving it."

"Correct," Astolfo said. "You studies are bringing you to sound ways of thinking. The voice must be given over to another entity with some power of speech. It must lodge within an animal that possesses a voice-box of its own. A magpie might be useful in this regard or a pet monkey. Mutano believes that Castilio has preserved his voice in the throat of a lazy, red-orange cat he hath named Sunbolt."

"Why does he think so?"

"I know not how he came to this conclusion. He is privy to some intelligence I wot not of. It may have to do with a set of verses Castilio dispatched to Stellina, comparing some portion of her anatomy to one of the nobler virtues of his cat."

I drank off the mug and wiped my lips with the heel of my palm. My voice had returned to its normal state and I was regaining my composure. 'Tis an unsettling business, to be struck dumb in an instant, to be incapable of speech for no fathomable reason.

"I have a glimmering," I announced. "This method of capturing a voice recalls to me the conundrum of the twin children. Is there a treatise on the subject from the olden time or is this a new-minted conceit?"

"An amalgam of both is likeliest," Astolfo said. "You might look into Lariotti's little monograph on the geometrical diminishments of the musical tone *re*. That is all I can recall that might be of the slightest help."

"Thank you," I said. "I will inform Mutano that I stand ready at any time to aid him in his effort to reclaim his voice."

"You need not trouble," Astolfo said. "He counts you his accomplice already."

A result of my varied readings and of hearing of Mutano's quest had been to clarify my purblind musings in regard to the shadow of the twin children. Now it seemed probable to me that they were not lacking a shadow that ought to be present, but that the shadow already was present and was only concealed. Maestro Astolfo must have suspected this to be the case when he inquired whether any part of the visible shadow was darker or more pronounced than the other portions of it. I had observed that the central part was of a darker tint and that it exhibited the same general outline, in smaller state, as the outline of the whole.

The two children possessed two shadows, only one was contained within the other. These shadows must have clung together, then fused inseparably, shortly after the birth of the twins. My task would be to cleave them, to set one apart from the other, causing two to stand where one had stood.

I began to reason upon the undertaking, pacing up and down the flagstones of the library, then going out into the chill, damp weather the storm had delivered and tramping about in the wet grasses of the courtyard. I desired that the cold air would sharpen my wits.

Some shadows are uncleavable from their parent objects. If a thief take the shadow of a man on the instant of his being illuminated by a stroke of lightning, that shadow will ever seek out the presence of iron and fasten into its grain irremovably. The fashioners of ceremonial shields often elaborate these shadow-shapes into fanciful designs highly prized by their clients. Almost equally impossible is the task of cutting away the shadow of a carefree maiden standing in the shadow-dapple of a cherry tree. Yet it can be done by masters such as Astolfo.

As I thought upon the lightning-bred shade's attraction to iron, I recalled also the device of the nested boxes which had stolen away Mutano's voice. I remembered too the shadow-stain of the statue of Prester Vonnard and how it clung to the cobbles of a plaza. A scheme came to mind then, and I determined to trace it out on my own, telling Astolfo little until it came to conclusion. But since Mutano required my aid to further his design, I would entreat his aid on behalf of my own.

THE MORROW BROKE bright and water-sprent, sunlight gleaming from every grass blade and leaf tip. The dawn birds were hilarious and did not lessen the volubility of their choruses till midmorning. Mutano was in an easy temper too; he anticipated the regaining of his voice. My part in his plan was but small, yet it might endanger my person. I was to deliver to Castilio at his lodgings in the Haywain Inn an ugly insult and a jovial but urgent invitation to meet Mutano on the field of honor where they would settle all insuavity between them with the clash of sabers.

This much Mutano communicated to me in one of the rapid finger dialects that he and Astolfo habitually conversed in. I had gathered enough of it to comprehend instructions and simple explanations, - sometimes with the aid of ear-boxings to fructify my attention. The only real peril, so stated his thumb and third finger, was that Castilio might insert a dagger in my windpipe upon hearing the insult — a complicated phrase involving his mother, his uncle, a goat, an ape, and a pig — without staying for the challenge to duel Mutano.

I asked him about his odd choice of weapons, for of all the choices open to him — long knives, clubs, maces, broadswords, &c. — the saber was least advantageous; 'twas the blade he was less agile with. For answer he gave me one of his ear-wide, many-toothed grins.

In return, I requested his aid in a bit of simple carpentry to my design and also in transporting my devices to the house of Sativius. After momentary reflection, he agreed to fall in with me.

The hour in which Mutano insisted that I deliver his messages was deepest twilight. Uncommon gloomy 'twas, this tavern room of the Haywain with its scant half dozen tallow candles disposed diversely. Besides the object of my attention and myself, the only other persons here were a raddle-haired serving maid and a baldpate dotard seated by the cold fireplace, opposing himself at a chessboard. Castilio sat on a bench, sipping at a tankard and playing idly with an ivory-handled dirk of modest but ominous proportion. I sat at a table with a glass of canary, waiting for him to grow tired of his game and sheathe the blade. Finally he thrust it back into his sleeve.

I advanced to stand before him; and he looked up into my eyes with a gaze that was challenging but also incurious, the gaze of a man determined to fear nothing that fate flung in his way. When I reeled off the insult entailing his complex ancestry and his dubious amatory practices, his expression did not change at first. Then he laughed, and when I heard that soft, insidious chuckle with its flat intonation, I understood why Mutano so loathed him and why all the world gave wide berth to his presence.

"You are but a parrot sent to prattle words not your own," he said. He looked away from my face into the far corner of the room. "Which of my foes has dispatched you here? Torpius? Scudator? Mutano? Master Thistledown?"

I handed over the document and he broke the seal. Murmuring the phrases as he read, he went through it carefully, poring over each syllable.

Now I took advantage of his distracted attention to lift the left edge of my cloak and let drop onto the table behind me the shadow of Creeper, the coiled mass which had traveled clinging to my doublet as I walked half across the expanse of Tardocco. Shadows, though they possess mass, are weightless, yet when I let go Creeper's umbra I felt that a burden had departed my body.

Castilio laid down the challenge missive. "How is it that Mutano delivereth not this foolhardy piece of effrontery in his own person?" he asked. "Why must he send forth a hireling?"

The truth was that Mutano, even now while I engaged the thoughts of his nemesis, was in Castilio's rooms above, searching for any receptacle that might contain his purloined voice. I sought to occupy his enemy's attention as long as possible. "I am no inconsequential menial," I replied, "but the confidential aide to Meastro Astolfo whose name is widely known."

"He is known as a prating, elderly thief who has narrowly escaped the gallows a score of times. I care not what title he has hung upon you, for a glance tells me you are but a furrow-slave with the mud of the turnip field still clinging to your soles — and to your soul."

"Mutano conceived that a challenge when delivered by a third party acquires more dignity and weight."

He rose abruptly and I knew his suspicions had been alerted. "You may tell Mutano that his challenge has been accepted in all particulars, including those of weapons choice, and field of honor and hour of combat."

I bowed. "I will say what you have said."

"Do so, though it may be I shall see him myself before you do." With these words, he brushed past me and strode toward the stairs by the entrance door. I knew that he expected, perhaps hoped, to find Mutano in his rooms.

"Is that the whole of your message?"

He did not reply but only bounded to the door at the top and flung it open and rushed into the corridor. I was pleased to see that Creeper's shadow leapt down from the table behind me and glided along at a distance from Castilio's heels. The time seemed opportune for me to depart also. If Castilio found his lodging ransacked, he would be down the stair with naked blade and unpleasant demeanor. I laid down coin for the canary, went out into the dark, wet street and betook me to the safety of Astolfo's manse. There I waited in the armchair, watching the dim orange pulse of dying embers of hearth-fire until I dozed away.

His search had proved fruitless, Mutano told Astolfo with a flurry of finger waggling. He had looked into the three small rooms of Castilio's lodging and found no place a voice might be stored away.

"No stoppered flasks or bottles?" Astolfo asked.

Mutano signed *No.*

"No small boxes or casques, as for jewels or coins or gilt buckles?"

None.

"Tell us then what you did see there. Omit nothing and try to recall all."

Mutano named articles of apparel, various handkerchiefs, a few gold eagles and lesser coins, spurs, &c. Boots beneath the bed, a woman's scarf draped over a chair back.

"Naught else?"

Mutano shrugged and signed unenthusiastically that a large, orange cat of melancholy, surly mien had watched him plundering about without so much as a tail twitch.

"This cat," Astolfo asked, "was he not disturbed by the shadow of Creeper that you deposited in the room?"

I was surprised. I had not known that we had set

two of the black one's shadows upon Castilio. This second one that Mutano let free would be a secondary, since I had brought the primary shadow into the tavern room. Whatever the purpose of this secondary, the conceit of the two shadows was clever, I thought.

Mutano signaled that the orange cat had seemed to take no notice of the shadow. In fact, it behaved, in not behaving at all, unlike any other feline he had met in his long acquaintance with the race.

"A human appurtenance, the voice of stout Mutano, has been affixed to its physiognomy," Astolfo said. "Having thieved away your voice, Castilio has managed to lodge it in this cat, I know not how. Such an addition to its nature will change the character of the beast at its foundation. For long and long, philosophers have conjectured what a cat would say could human vocality be conferred upon it. Many of the graybeards averred that it would say nothing at all, lest it reveal some of the secrets of its mysterious race. It seemeth, in the instance of Castilio's cat, at least, that their suspicion proved true."

"How then may its human voice be captured?" I asked.

"Oh, we have already prepared our voice-trap," Astolfo said. "It is constructed along the pattern of Castilio's nested wooden boxes, only ours is an intricate horn of silver and ivory, in appearance like a twisted ear trumpet. There is no doubt that it will capture the utterance-essence of a voice and keep it safely."

"I mean, how will Mutano take back his voice if the cat does not speak?"

They exchanged glances. Mutano seemed a trifle apprehensive.

"Risks must be run," Astolfo said. "In the first place, Castilio's cat now possesses two voices, one of them proper to itself. If its own voice is dominant within it, then it will make only sounds ordinary to a cat. But if Mutano's voice has gained — so to speak — the upper hand, then it will speak out in his voice and that one will become prisoner of our trumpet-device."

"But why should it speak at all, since its best advantage — or Castilio's — lies in keeping silent?"

"We will put to it the question that, when asked directly, every feline must answer by force of its inner nature."

"What is this question?"

"We shall ask this Sunbolt if he be truly the King of the Cats. If he be King, he will rise hissing, all hackles and claws, and bound away in a flash, leaving behind a smell as of brimstone and burning roses. If he hath not been designated the royalty of its feline world, then he is constrained to respond, *Nay, not yet.*"

"This is but an old tale to amuse children in the chimney corner," I said. "I was no taller than a milking stool when first I heard it. Even the most unlearned of hay-foot villagers is wiser than to credit it. 'Tis a moldy stuff indeed."

Mutano's wide grin forewarned me that I had overstepped the bounds of my knowledge.

"Apply your noddle," Astolfo said. "When has it come about that the hay no longer graces your buskins? If every instance of the elder lore were false, the land would have been depopulated generations ago. Why do you doubt what I tell you?"

Since I had lately been reading in Lord Verulam's *Novum organon,* I ventured to speculate that this interrogation of cats must have been rarely put to the test; otherwise, there would be voluminous testimonia in the writings of the sages. " 'Tis by making experiment that we discover truth and falsity," I said. "There must be by our time many thousands of younglings who have put that question to their dear pusses and have received for reply only uncomprehending disregard."

"Too easy an interpretation to offer," said Astolfo. "How many of the felines so queried have been accoutered with a human voice?"

"Few," I admitted.

"Do you not think it likely that cats communicate among themselves with recondite signs and significations?"

"Perhaps."

"Would you be able to cipher out the language of a cat's ears and tail?"

"I could not."

"Then you may ask, for all the remainder of your years, of every animal you meet whether it is King of the Cats and receive continual denials and never know of it because you lack the key to their language. Is this not so?"

"It may be so."

"Let us hear no more of the foolishness of the old tales. We owe much of our new physic to the simples of farm wives and much of our knowledge of the skies to watchful shepherds. Since you desire to experiment, after the manner of Verulam, it shall be your duty to put the question to Castilio's cat."

"My duty? How can that come about? Castilio knows me and will take care that I do not depart a next encounter unscathed. How am I to evade his enmity?"

"Tomorrow at the noon hour he will be engaged in a duel with Mutano in the graveyard atop Mount Windscaur in the northern precinct of the town, a good half league distant from the Haywain Inn. Then you may enter his rooms, put the question to Sunbolt, and bring away with you Mutano's voice which you shall have captured in the chambered spirals of the silver trumpet. Also you are to gather the two shadows of Creeper which ought to be present there."

"Shall he not have suspected a design against him and have posted a confederate to guard his belongings?"

"That would present a difficulty your ingeniousness must overcome."

"I do not comprehend why we have set upon him two shadows of Creeper," I said. "Our plan as it stands does not require their presence."

"It is as useful as 'tis rare to have animate shadows in one's employ," Astolfo said. "If 'twere only to train them to an exercise, that would be value enough."

"Well, I will perform this commission," I said, "but I should like to exact some payment for it, some just return for my trouble, so that I can fulfill my obligations to the family Sativius, for I have formed, methinketh, an artifice that may help to resolve the affair."

"What have you conceived?"

When I began to list my necessities — the blue mirror, the sheet of transparent glass, the vials of silver salt, &c. — I saw that Mutano looked at me with an expression of full surprise. I considered it a victory to have startled my raw-knuckle tutor who so continuously regarded me as an addlehead ploughboy. Astolfo smiled knowingly, however, and murmured an unintelligible phrase about "membraneous effusion." He acquiesced to my requests for materials and promised that Mutano would aid me in my endeavor.

JUST BEFORE NOON on the morrow, I placed myself around the corner across the cobbles from the Haywain so that I might see while standing concealed. In time a groom led round a black, mettlesome mare with black leathers to the front and Castilio came out. He snatched the bridle from the lad and seemed to wish to bark at him an imprecation, yet no sound issued when he opened his mouth. He was in foul temper, all out of sorts with the bright day that had followed the rainy hours. He mounted and jogged crisply away, saber flapping against his thigh as he plied more spur than necessary.

I tarried a while longer, observing all that I could, and then entered the inn and made my way unhindered to Castilio's rooms. All was just as it had been before, except that the female scarf was absent. No drawer was locked, no door bolted. The man seemed to invite inspection of his every article and, finding things thus, I went cursorily about the business, then turned my attention to matters feline.

First, I ascertained the whereabouts of the two shadows of Creeper, the primary dark one that had nestled beneath the neatly dressed bed and then the lighter secondary that crouched inside an overturned boot. In a cushioned chair by the window sat orange Sunbolt that Mutano had found here and described in detail. There was no mistaking this large tom with its subtle stripes of slightly yellow tint. It dozed, with feet tucked under and eyes almost completely shut. But the movement of its ears indicated awareness of a stranger in the vicinity.

Here now was the moment of revelation. I had always been curious to conjecture what Mutano's voice would sound like, he being so large of corpus and saturnine of temperament. Would it not boom out like a tympanum? Or might it thunder and reverberate like an empty tun rolled down a tall flight of wooden stairs? Perhaps in issuing from the voice-box of this cat, it would roar forth like some tiger of the night.

I placed myself before the animal, produced our trumpet device and turned the wide bell toward it, keeping the cork-lined round of parchment stopper in my right hand ready to seal the aperture once the sound entered into the tapering silver labyrinth. Then I put to it the question it could not evade:

"Art thou King of the Cats?"

It opened its green, agate-hard eyes and elevated its hindquarters and gave a mighty stretch with its forepaws, seeming to extend to the lengthiest every ligament and fiber of muscle in its thorax. It yawned its widest. Then it resettled itself into its former posture, turned its wedgy face upward and said:

"Nay. The hour is not yet."

I clapped the stopper in, wondering already if I had held the device in horizontal position aright and in sufficient proximity to the cat's mouth. I had tried to make no sound that would obstruct the passage of the words through the æther or adulterate them with an extraneity.

Naught was left to do now but to gather the two shadows of Creeper into the inner folds of my shagreen cloak and march back home across Tardocco. I intended to set a leisurely pace, for there was much to think on.

Mutano's voice was not orotund and commanding, as I had supposed, but rang out a clear, lyrical treble.

Astolfo had avouched that he was a musical man, but that disclosure had not prepared me for the peculiar sweetness of tone and the light, reedy vibrato that were so winning in timbre. Had the cat's vocal physiognomy altered Mutano's own, to make it so dulcet? I have endured the amorous lays of cats in the midnight hours with small patience and have found none of them seductive. Whimsically, I pictured Mutano in a form feline, slinking out under a great buttery moon and entreating his lady love in harmonious cadenza and receiving as a melodious refusal his own terse rebuttal: *"Nay, the hour is not yet."*

"THESE DUELS CONSUME a tiresome portion of the clock," Astolfo said to me when I returned.

The three of us had lately formed the habit of occupying the small library. In time past we had gathered most often in the great kitchen, but the scullery staff and the two cooks complained that we were too often present when they had tasks in hand. For his part, Astolfo would rarely gainsay his chief cook; that artisan was necessary, he claimed, for the conduct of financial affairs.

"I had not expected that Mutano would return till near twilight," I said. I leaned forward in a strap-bottomed chair and watched the two shadows of Creeper gambol together in the far corner of the room. He, the parent of the umbrae, was nowhere to be seen. Lately, Creeper had been known to sleep for days on end, rousing only to tend to the demands of gut and bowel. It was explained to me that the drawing off of two lively shadows from his form depleted his store of *vis vitae*; long sleeping aided return of it.

"These two, Mutano and Castilio are acting without seconds," Astolfo said, "and there is no need for elaborate protocol — and yet they will be long at the business, though the combat itself shall prolong for only swift-flying minutes."

"I marvel at his choice of weapons," I said, "for Mutano knoweth well that the saber is not the steel to which he is best accustomed."

"Perhaps his challenge is to himself, as well as to Castilio."

"He hazards his life. Is't not too risky a venture to gain so small a point of honor?"

"The rules and limits Mutano establishes for himself are unknown to me. It may be that if we apprehended them, his comportment would display a logic."

" 'Tis well beyond my fathoming."

"I see there in the corner the two shades of Creeper," Astolfo said. "I conclude then that you have brought off your part of the affair successfully."

"I cannot affirm yea or nay," I replied. "I followed my instructions to the iota of the letter closely as I could. Whether I managed to regain with our little trap Mutano's voice, I cannot say. If so I did, then it is here." I reached behind my chair and produced the trumpet-like contraption.

Astolfo then required me to give a full account of all that took place and broke off my narrative when I told of entering the room. "Pray do not leap to the middle," he said. "Did you take heed that Castilio had already departed?"

I hastened to assure him that I had kept watch until he had mounted for his appointment and had kept at my post for some little time afterward.

"You observed him to come out and take the reins?"

"I did."

"How did his demeanor appear to you — in comparison, I mean, with the way you found him two days ago in the tavern room?"

I closed me eyes to bring the picture clear to mind. "He seemed restless of spirit. In the tavern he looked all a piece of easy insolence, but coming out to meet Mutano, he looked somdel apprehensive. Certes, he was irritable, for he was harsh to his groom."

"It appeareth, then, that Creeper's shadows performed well their offices," Astolfo said. "They were set there to obstruct his breathing in the night, thus to prevent sound sleep. You have experienced this obstruction of inhalation by the cat's shadow, have you not?"

"I have."

"Out he came then, ill tempered and nervy, not so well fit to go at sabering . . . And when he had mounted?"

"Off he cantered, after a sharp spurring of the stallion's flanks." I went on to tell, at a calm pace, everything else that I had heard and seen and done, expressing my surprise at the sound of Mutano's voice as the cat spoke its sentence to me. I tried to describe the peculiar sweetness of timbre and melodiousness of cadence.

"Have you ever stood in a wintry grove of trees with a cold wind scraping and rattling the bare limbs together so that they creaked and squealed?" Astolfo asked.

"Yes."

"That is how I recall the sound of Mutano's voice. None of this consort of musical tones that you speak of, but an eldritch grating almost to stand one's neck hairs on end."

"I will avouch for what I heard. You told me before that he was a sometime minstrel."

"His speaking voice was quite unmusical. It may be that this is a peculiarly musical cat and that his native talents wrought a happy change upon Mutano's vocal qualities in his ordinary speaking. We may hope this to be the case, for the other explanation is less sanguine."

"How so?"

"A man who performs so audacious a theft as that of another man's voice will not be content to perform the deed a single time only. It may be that this o'ersugared voice you heard belongeth to another than Mutano and that his is placed in another receptacle. Would you think that the voice you heard from the cat might have been purloined from a woman?"

I thought upon it. "I should not say so. For all its harmoniousness, it lacked a certain softness we associate with the fair."

"We shall not know what is certain for some small space of time," Astolfo said. "Perhaps you will tell now what progress you have made in the affair of the Sativius family."

"I shall describe a contrivance I have imagined, a complicated arrangement of mirrors and sheets of glass. I cannot effect the portage of these elements alone and will ask Mutano's aid."

"He is in your debt."

"So I have expected. I shall desire him to help to move and position these glasses." I rose and walked to a long library table and returned with a large square of paper. "Here I have drawn out my plans, if you should care to see them over."

Astolfo took the crowded page with an air of lazy amusement, looked at it, and began turning it side-wise and topsy-turvy. "You make up your designs with great enthusiasm," he commented. Soon, though, he commenced to study my scribbles and hatchings with care, humming a tuneless ditty. He spent a good-ish deal of time examining the sheet before rolling it into a cylinder and laying it across his lap. "These conceits you have laid out here — do they originate in your brain or found you them in some treatise tucked away in our shelves?"

"They are mine."

He nodded. "The pride of your tone assures me. I ask the question because of the coincident nature of your imaginings."

"In what way?"

He held up the page. "The designs you have made are similar in many respects to the methods that Mutano and I employed to animate the shades of Creeper."

"I have no knowledge of how that was done and, as you can see, I have no ambitions to create shadows of independent force and motion. I would not care to animate the children's umbrae, only to separate them one from another."

"It is your notion then that the twins do each possess a shadow and that one is contained inside the other?"

"Yes."

"And you propose with this arrangement of glasses to separate the two shadows so that they will then attach to their proper casters?"

"That is my plan." I waited with some wariness for his sentence upon my constructions. I could hardly expect him to applaud them; but if he disallowed Mutano to work in my behalf, I would have to begin once again; and he had warned me that time was rapidly shortening before a sad fate befell the young ones.

"It seemeth sound so far as it reaches," he said. "I might suggest a few improving touches, if they will not injure your pride or damage your project as you see it."

"I welcome any advice of Maestro Astolfo." I made a teasing half bow from my seated position.

"My advice must wait," he said, "for Mutano has returned, I believe."

In strode he. His complexion was flushed, his eyes glary, yet he wore one of his monstrous, widemouthed grins. A line of spattered blood dotted his tunic from the collar down to the last button, but I could tell it was not his own.

"Welcome," said Astolfo.

In reply, Mutano tossed upon the small table between us a bloody codpiece I recognized as belonging to Castilio.

Astolfo AND I were not to hear the sound of Mutano's voice — if indeed he had acquired a voice — for some little time because he took himself aside to spend long hours in company with the capture instrument, inhaling or imbibing, as 'twere, his own voice from its convolutions. We surmised that vocal experimenting engaged him, that he was exercising his throat in private, and that he would reveal the result whenas he list.

It was with surprising good grace in the meantime

that he submitted to my desires in service of the Sativius family, helping me to transport my apparatus across the city, into the household, and up the stair to the room with the bay window's light. Horseface Graysmock watched us arrange the pieces with undisguised disfavor. I rather hoped she would bestow some disdaining remark upon Mutano. He had no patience with females of her strain and would send her sprawling with the back of his hand did she once overstep.

The *schema* was disposed thus:

I) The long table before the window was removed and the children brought forward toward the light;

II) the pair stood close together to cast a shadow behind;

III) directly posterior to them a large sheet of transparent glass was mounted, so that the shadow of the children fell on it complete;

IV) this glass was framed all around with a molding of purest copper;

V) the glass itself had been dusted over with a light coating of a silver salt that allowed the shadows to pass through

VI) to a mirror behind the silvery glass:

VII) which mirror was made of a peculiar glass tinted dark blue that had the power of absorbing images deeply, pulling them far into itself.

Sativius and Funisia gazed with apprehension upon this tri-fold arrangement. The father was very particular in inquiring whether Maestro Astolfo was aware of what I had projected and if he approved. I assured him that Astolfo knew all and had contributed wise advice of optical nature. Funisia welcomed any venture that might benefit her brood.

As I instructed the twins that they must stand very still for quite a little while, they only stared mutely into my face, as if trying to read not only my intentions but any trace of doubt my mind might harbor. I murmured softly as I stood them in compliance with my design. When I was satisfied that the images of the shadows passed through the dusted glass into the mirror, I made a finger sign to Mutano who stood at the side of the glass. He produced a piece of electrum about the size of his palm, took from his belt pouch a small patch of lynx fur, and then rubbed it over the electrum. When he had rubbed for a short time, he touched the electrum to the copper molding of the mirror. This action he performed continuously as I observed, standing to one side and facing away from the light, the shadow of the pair as it fell upon the dusted glass and the image of the children as it entered the blue mirror.

This process required the better part of an hour and I tried not to allow my apprehensions to ruffle my demeanor. If the children grew restless and moved about, the silvered shadow would be blurred, the darker core more difficult to distinguish from the outer penumbra. If Mutano grew impatient, flung the lump of amber at my head, and stalked from the house, all would be ruined. If my scheme proved ineffective, if the spark from the rubbed electrum did not transfer itself through the salt across the pane in sufficient force to animate the more passive shadow that was absorbed as the core of the other, I would again be a figure of ridicule to Astolfo and Mutano and must endure their humors and rude satires for a long time to come. And when again would Astolfo entrust me a commission to work upon alone?

At last there occurred a change in the shadow in the glass. The dark core grew lighter in tint and extended its shape until it was almost identical in size with its envelope. In the blue mirror the images of the twins grew more distinct, their outlines more sharply defined. When the inner and outer shadows verged closely on identity in size and density, I sharply bade the children to stand apart, to go quickly to the places I had marked on the carpet with two linen handkerchiefs.

I was jubilant at the success of my experiment, but my joy immediately gave way to chagrin as the boy Rudens became even paler than before. His face drained of all color and he fell to the floor. I rushed to him, arriving at his side even before his mother arrived, and put my ear to his face. His breath came but faintly and I asked for water to bathe his face and hands. He stirred a little at the touch of the water but did not open his eyes. Seeing this, Funisia gathered him up and bore him away.

Graysmock ran over to accuse me. "You have killed him! You have murdered the young master!"

"Silence your tongue," I said. "No real harm has come to him. Go prepare a strong effusion of ginger root and give it to him when he wakens from sleep."

She left in silent fury, and Sativius knelt to Rudensia. She appeared to me much less affected by the splitting of the shadow than her brother had been, yet it was obvious that she had felt a change rush upon her. Her father peered into her eyes, then clasped her tightly to his chest. "Is it so?" he asked. "Have my children each a shadow now?"

"It is so," I replied. "The effect of the division is less strong for Rudensia because what was taken from her was not correctly hers in the first place. For the boy, the sudden accession of his shadow overpowered him with a feeling that something long lost had been wholly returned. His was the lesser, darker umbra that Rudensia's had overtaken in their earliest hours. We have been fortunate in our day of restoration. Had it occurred later, we might have lost one or both of the twins." I went on to explain, as Astolfo had explained to me, that if once their souls entwined, they must face either the doom of madness as their spirits melted together into one or of physical death if ever they had to be separate one from the other.

He stood, still embracing the girl in his right arm. "I do not comprehend these matters," he said. "I am but a blunt man of business and all this spider-web machination with shadows only perplexes."

"That is because you are unaccustomed. Think with what bewilderment a ploughboy looks upon a ship as it weighs anchor and steers from harbor. All will seem but arrant confusion to him, with sailors darting here and yon and the masters bawling orders and the sheets tying off and the cables laid by, but to your practiced eye all the commotion is of a pattern and every action is demanded by a necessity. It is the same with shadows. One must learn the ropes."

"I believe the fee you set was two hundred eagles," he said. "If my son revive in sound health, as you say that he shall, I will add another fifty."

"That is unlooked for," I said. *"The fee is set and to be met,* as the saying goes. Only do make certain that Horseface carries out her duties in good order and all shall be well."

"Horse—?"

"Please pardon me. I meant no offense. The term rose unbidden to my lips."

"As it sometime has to my thoughts." He smiled. "Yet she is fitting in her office, though imperfect in manner. Nevertheless, she shall see that you are offered wine and cake before you depart."

"I thank your kind courtesy, but I must hasten to other duties. Maestro Astolfo always has several affairs in hand and I seem always to lag behind the order of his requests. If you will dispatch the eagles to him by messenger, along with a letter favoring or disfavoring my labors here, as you see fit, we shall be obliged."

"That is soon done," he said, "and again I tender my gratitude. I shall fully commend your execution of the matter."

With the usual bows and flourishing of my short cloak, I took leave.

THERE WAS TO BE a petite fete of celebration for the three of us, marking a success in my first unguided excursion into sciomantic venture. We hoped also to be celebrating the return of Mutano's voice, but he had so far kept silent in our company. He had, in fact, kept apart from us for long stretches. We surmised that he was exercising his throat; the voice of a man of his make, confined for a long period in the voice-box of a cat, must have suffered diminution, if not deterioration. Astolfo suggested that he might be practicing an aria supple and trillful to amaze us.

The cook had told the steward to lay out our supper on a corner of the long table in the dining room, but Astolfo would not have it. The rains had returned, and he desired the closeness of the kitchen with its oven heat and lamplight glancing from the surfaces of burnished copper and polished crystal. He was punctilious upon the victuals too: turbot and cold veal, varied herbage, a roast of venison, and then an apple tart with a great wedge of cheese from my native province. Topery would include cider and beer and a bottle of wine, aged and heady.

He and I sat at the table the steward had brought in and sipped at draughts of cider whilst we waited for Mutano to appear.

As I expected, Astolfo used the time to ask sharp questions about the Sativius children and my procedure in dividing the shadows. I described in detail every stage of preparation, every step of the process, and every piece of apparatus. During my peroration, he smiled at certain passages, closed his eyes and appeared to meditate during others. When I concluded, he pressed his fingertips together and considered silently for a space. Then: "I will say it is to your credit that you appear to have discovered, by strength of your own wit, another of the traditional methods of taking shadows."

I tried not to show that I was a little crestfallen. "Then this method was known already?"

He blinked his gray eyes and slowly rested them upon mine. "The world was here long before you and I scuffed its soil with our boots. There were mages of great mentation who came before, rank on serried rank. Much of the lore they gained has been devoured by time. If we had it in its greater bulk, we should feel ourselves as small in comparison to them as scurrying voles."

by Fred Chappell   173

"Hath this method I thought mine own a name?"

"*Severing* you know as the term for the thieving of a shadow surreptitiously, without the awareness of its caster. *Sundering* you know as when a shadow is taken by violence, raped away from the parent object. *Surrendering* we call it when a person voluntarily gives over a shadow to the purposes of another. You have discovered without the aid of instruction the process of *seduction,* wherein the shade is lured from the parent object and leaves it gradually by force of attraction to another object or under its own volition."

"You have before now hinted that shadows might possess minds and wills independent," I said. "I do not see how this can be."

"Yet you might have tried another 'experiment,' as you call it and then come to a different turn of mind."

"How so?"

"Your procedure is so ingenious and so complicated that I hesitate to describe this one other method. After your machinations, it will seem but puerile."

"In the instance of children, that one most confident in the love of its parents, or of one of them, will have the stronger shadow and it shall absorb the weaker. You yourself observed that Rudensia's mother gave her a caress habitual, without thinking. Her shade was the stronger."

"That is a simpler and less expensive method of division," I admitted. "Still, I believe that mine would more impress the paterfamilias."

"I must agree," Astolfo said. "But yours had a large element of danger. When you profused the shadow in the silvered glass with energetic spark, you were fortunate that it did not acquire enough *vis* to escape on its own and leave our child bereft."

"That is why I told Mutano to smash the glass upon the precise instant."

He nodded. "Yes, you had that forethought, at least — and having spoken of him, we have summoned his presence."

Mutano entered the kitchen with something of a swagger in his march, came to the table and gazed down upon the viands with hearty pleasure. He smiled upon Astolfo and me, as beamingly as if he first saw us upon returning from a wearisome journey.

"Now we are complete," Astolfo said, "and the occasion is meet for the proposal of toasts. Falco, if you will but pour Mutano a healthy measure —"

I poured the good beer into his mug.

"— I will begin by congratulating our younger friend upon his triumph in an enterprise of his own."

We drank and refilled and I raised my glass in Mutano's direction. "And Mutano must be feted. He has made it certain, without taking the man's life, that Castilio will never again despoil young maidens or steal away the paramours of others. I present also my grateful thanks for his aid at the house of Sativius."

We drank and refilled and Mutano pointed his glass toward Astolfo and me in turn. He cleared his throat officiously, took a deep breath, and said in three melodious tones:

"Miaou."   ❧

The author tells us. "When the characters of shadow-master Astolfo, the neophyte shadow-thief Falco, and the hulking, mute manservant Mutano appeared unbidden in my mind, I had not thought how Mutano came to be without power of speech. Then one evening as I looked upon our taciturn cat Eugenia ("Oogie"), it occurred to me that someone had stolen his voice — just as cats have been said to steal the breath from persons on the verge of death.

Then I wrote the story.

Five times.

www.ingramcontent.com/pod-product-compliance
Lightning Source LLC
Chambersburg PA
CBHW052134170626
46812CB00004B/1399